INDIANA JONES™

AND THE ARMS OF GOLD

PART 4

STORY
LEE MARRS

ART
LEO DURAÑONA

COLORS
MATTHEW HOLLINGSWORTH

LETTERS
STEVE HAYNIE

COVER ART
RUSSELL WALKS

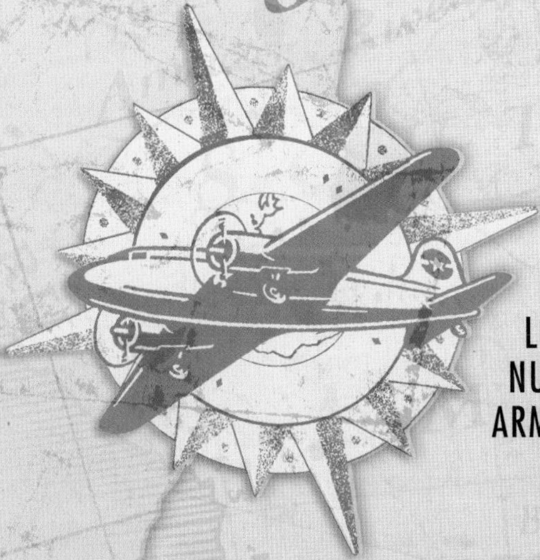

RESEARCH, REFERENCE,
AND TRANSLATIONS
LOREN McINTYRE, JANE ANDERSON NUÑEZ, DR. ANNE MARCHANT, DIEGO ARMUS, DAVE FOGARTY, MAL WARWICK, and DAVID STALEY

Spotlight

DARK HORSE COMICS

VISIT US AT
www.abdopublishing.com

Reinforced library bound edition published in 2011 by Spotlight, a division of the ABDO Group, 8000 West 78th Street, Edina, Minnesota 55439. Spotlight produces high-quality reinforced library bound editions for schools and libraries. Published by agreement with Dark Horse Comics, Inc., and Lucasfilm Ltd.

Printed in the United States of America, Melrose Park, Illinois.
052010
092010
This book contains at least 10% recycled materials.

Library of Congress Cataloging-in-Publication Data

Marrs, Lee.
Indiana Jones and the arms of gold / story [by] Lee Marrs ; art [by] Leo Duranona. -- Reinforced library bound ed.
p. cm. -- (Indiana Jones and the arms of gold ; v. 1-4)
Summary: The intrepid archaeologist Indiana Jones travels to Argentian to seek a lost Incan treasure.
ISBN 978-1-59961-757-2 (vol. 1) -- ISBN 978-1-59961-758-9 (vol. 2) -- ISBN 978-1-59961-759-6 (vol. 3) -- ISBN 978-1-59961-760-2 (vol. 4)
1. Graphic novels. [1. Graphic novels 2. Adventure and adventurers--Fiction. 3. Incas--Antiquities--Fiction. 4. Indians of South America--Antiquities--Fiction. 5. Argentina--Fiction.] I. Durañona, ill. II. Title.
PZ7.7.M35Ind 2010
741.5'973--dc22

2009052830

Spotlight

All Spotlight books have reinforced library bindings and are manufactured in the United States of

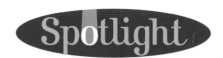

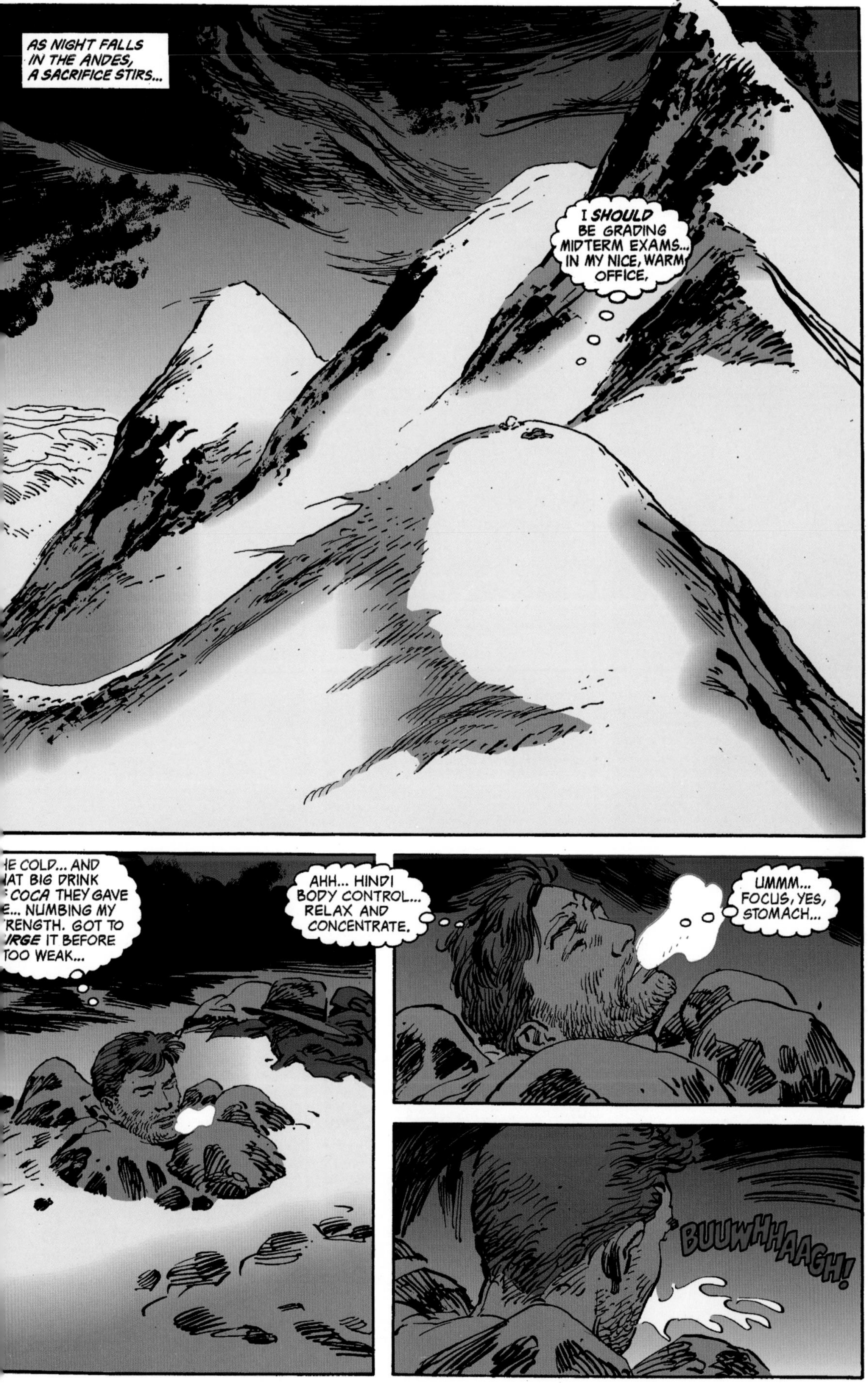
AS NIGHT FALLS IN THE ANDES, A SACRIFICE STIRS...
I SHOULD BE GRADING MIDTERM EXAMS... IN MY NICE, WARM OFFICE.
HE COLD... AND IAT BIG DRINK COCA THEY GAVE E... NUMBING MY TRENGTH. GOT TO IRGE IT BEFORE TOO WEAK...
AHH... HINDI BODY CONTROL... RELAX AND CONCENTRATE.
UMMM... FOCUS, YES, STOMACH...
BUUWHHAAGH!

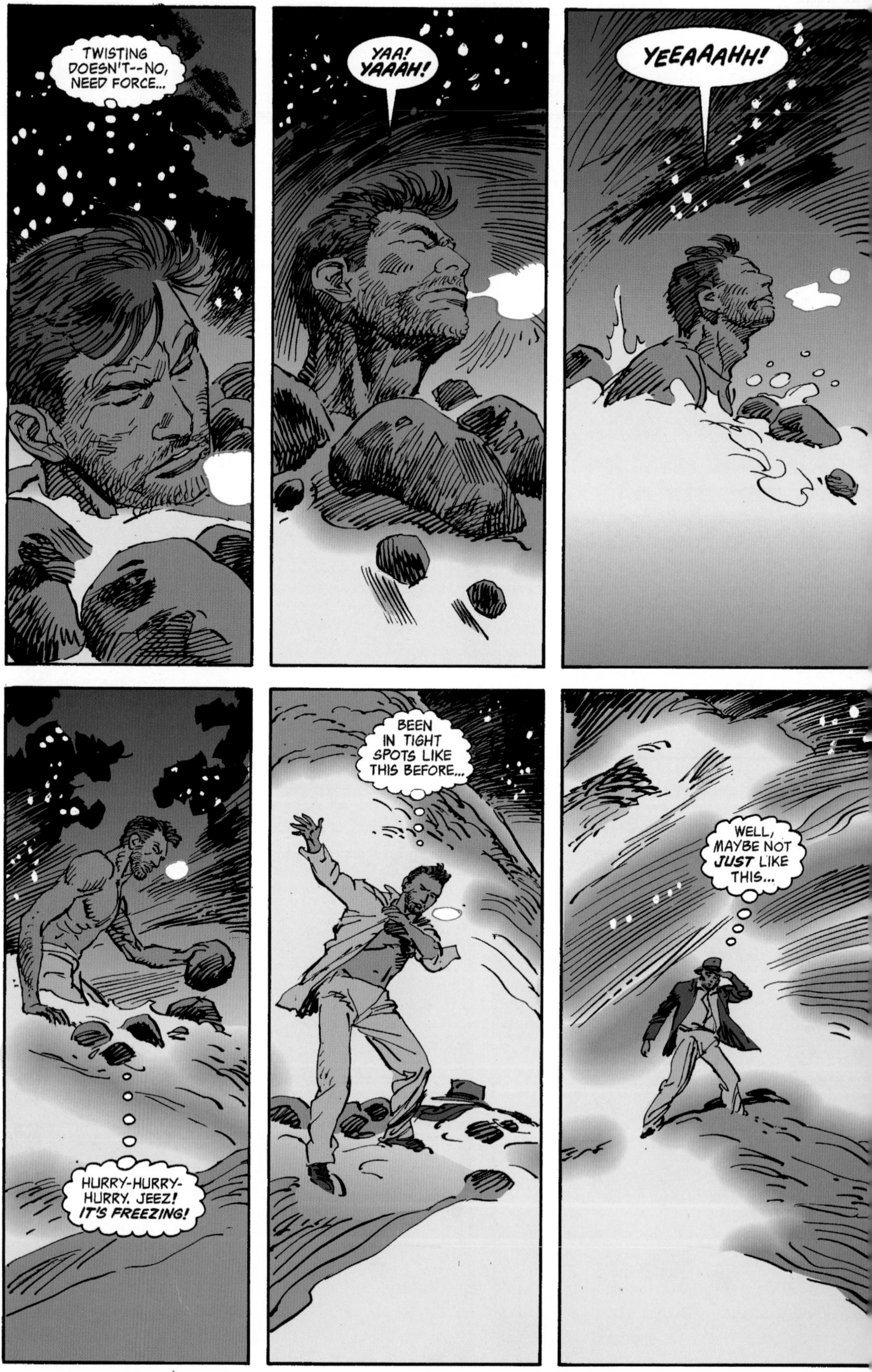
TWISTING DOESN'T--NO, NEED FORCE...
YAA! YAAAH!
YEEAAAAHH!
HURRY-HURRY-HURRY. JEEZ! IT'S FREEZING!
BEEN IN TIGHT SPOTS LIKE THIS BEFORE...
WELL, MAYBE NOT JUST LIKE THIS...

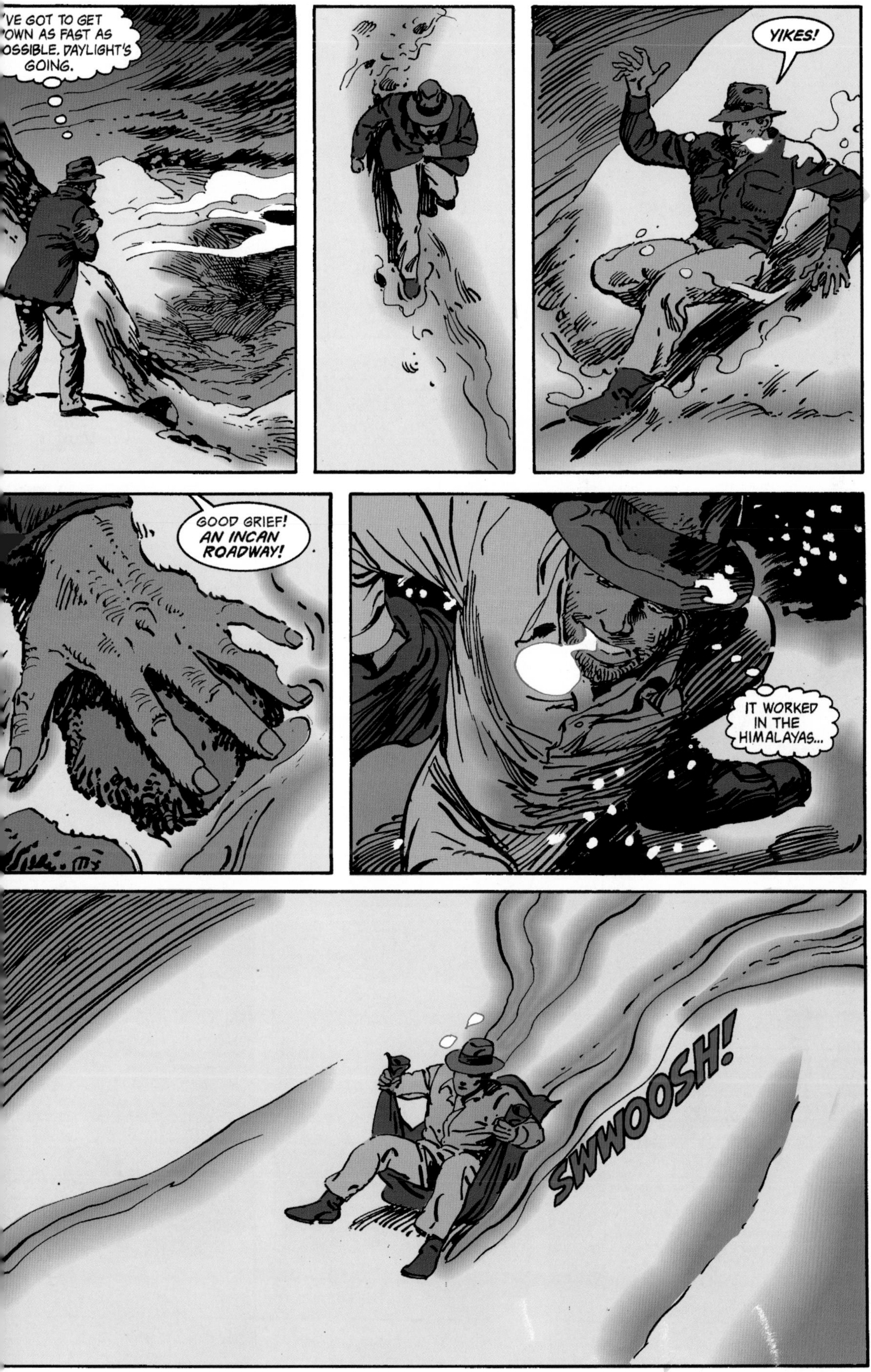
'VE GOT TO GET
OWN AS FAST AS
OSSIBLE. DAYLIGHT'S
GOING.
YIKES!
GOOD GRIEF!
AN INCAN
ROADWAY!
IT WORKED
IN THE
HIMALAYAS...
SWWOOSH!

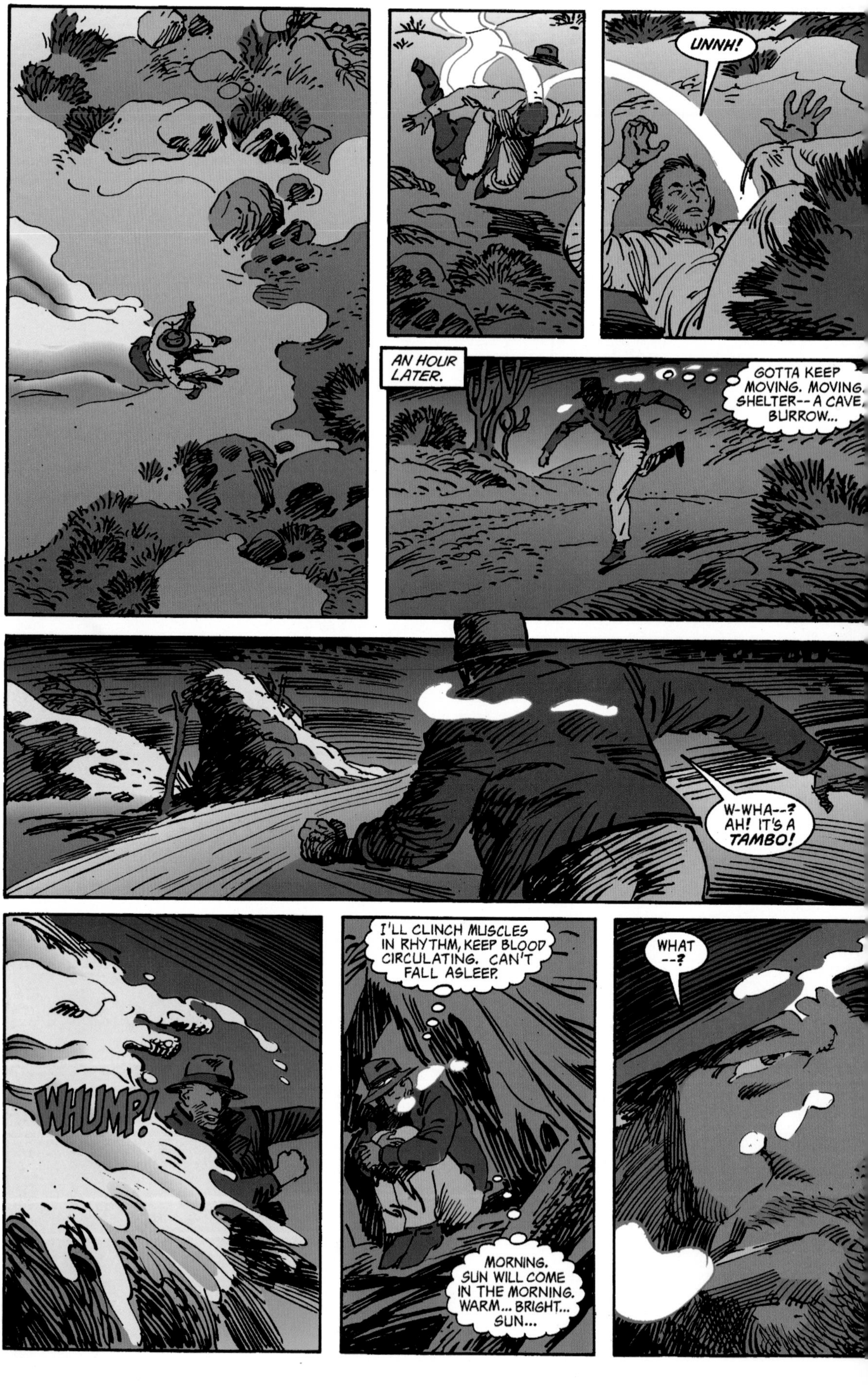
UNNH!
AN HOUR LATER.
GOTTA KEEP MOVING. MOVING. SHELTER-- A CAVE, BURROW...
W-WHA--? AH! IT'S A TAMBO!
WHUMP!
I'LL CLINCH MUSCLES IN RHYTHM, KEEP BLOOD CIRCULATING. CAN'T FALL ASLEEP.
MORNING. SUN WILL COME IN THE MORNING. WARM... BRIGHT... SUN...
WHAT --?

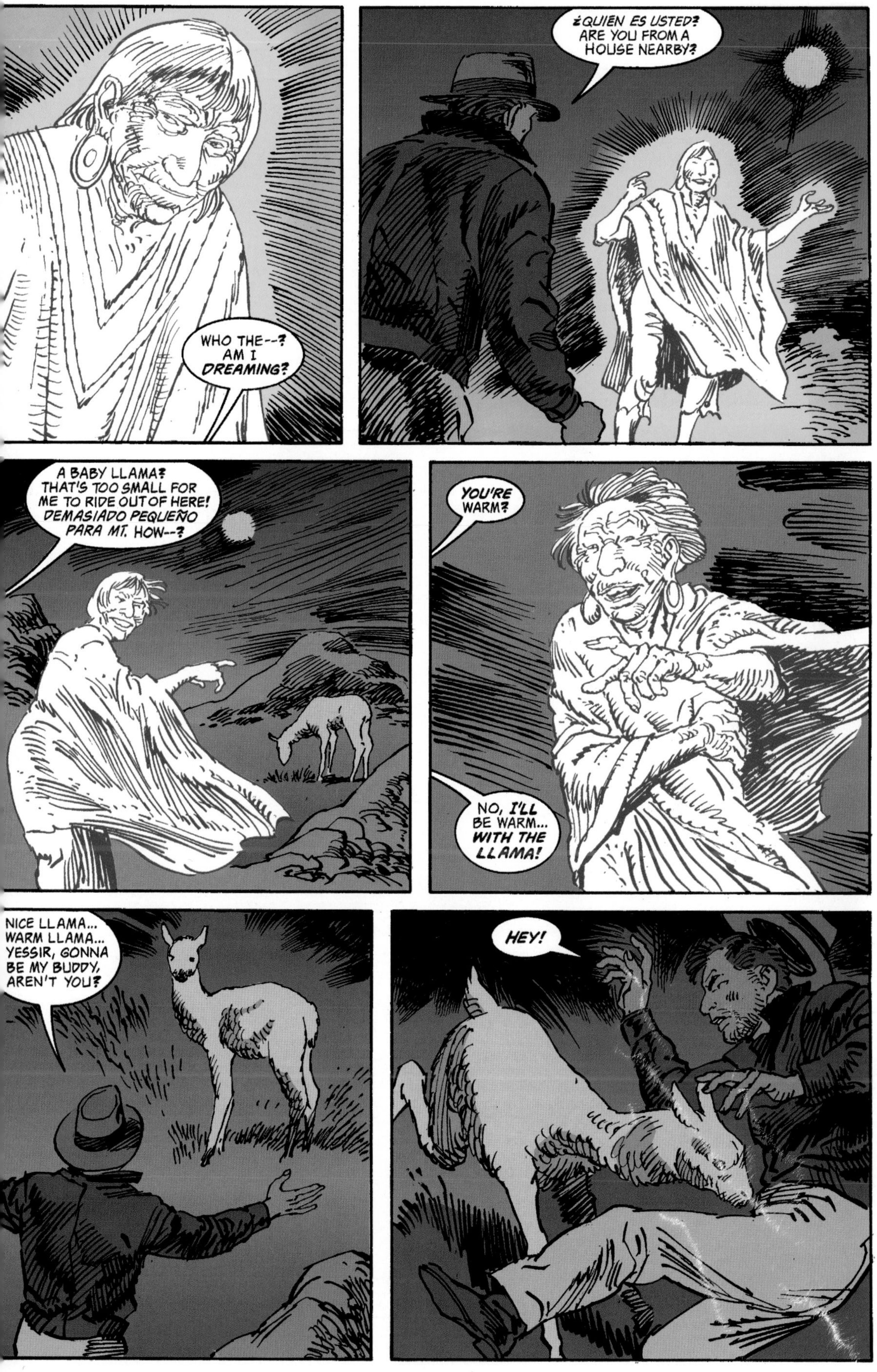
WHO THE--? AM I DREAMING?
¿QUIEN ES USTED? ARE YOU FROM A HOUSE NEARBY?
A BABY LLAMA? THAT'S TOO SMALL FOR ME TO RIDE OUT OF HERE! DEMASIADO PEQUEÑO PARA MI. HOW--?
YOU'RE WARM?
NO, I'LL BE WARM... WITH THE LLAMA!
NICE LLAMA... WARM LLAMA... YESSIR, GONNA BE MY BUDDY, AREN'T YOU?
HEY!

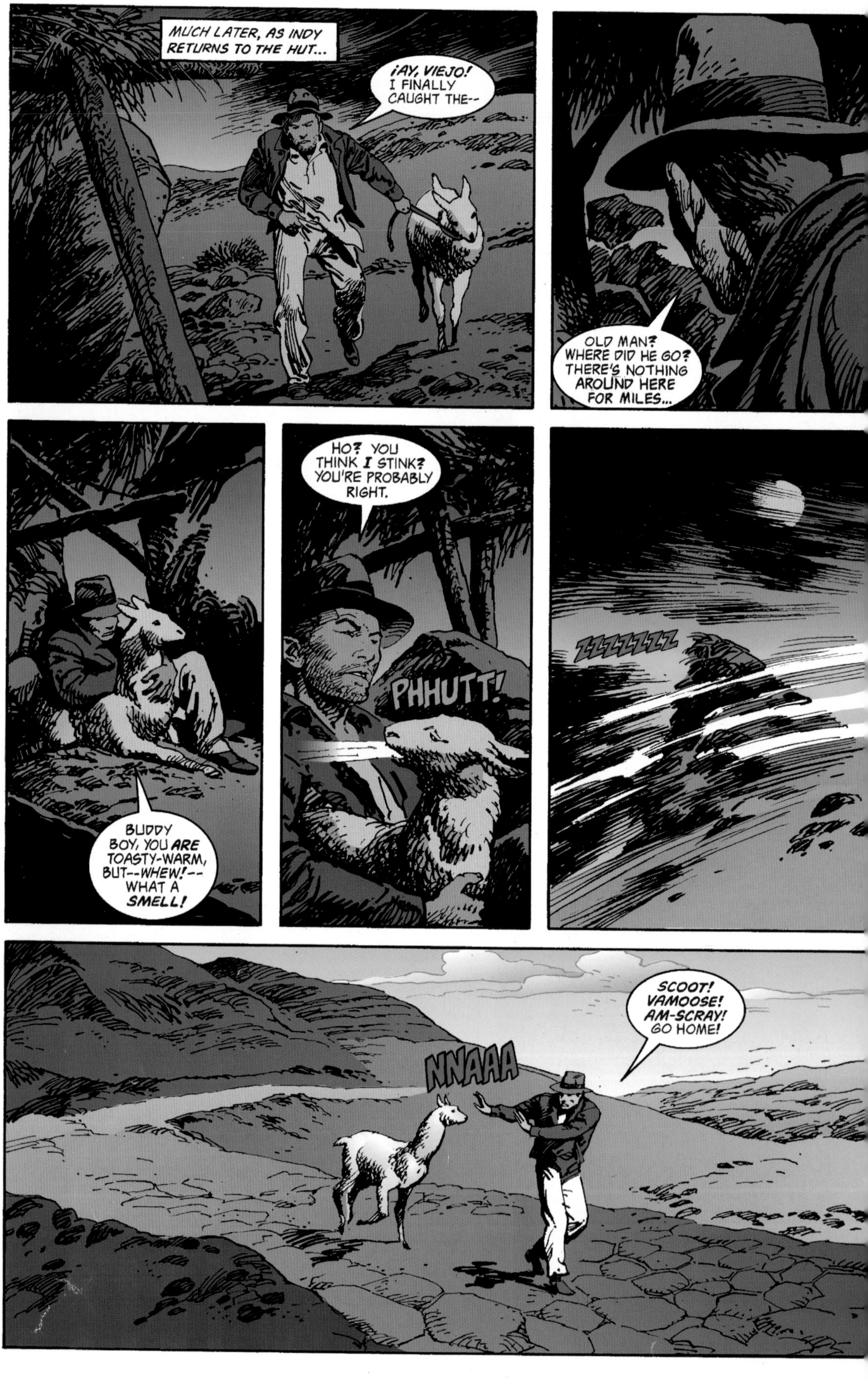
MUCH LATER, AS INDY RETURNS TO THE HUT...
¡AY, VIEJO! I FINALLY CAUGHT THE--
OLD MAN? WHERE DID HE GO? THERE'S NOTHING AROUND HERE FOR MILES...
BUDDY BOY, YOU ARE TOASTY-WARM, BUT--WHEW!--WHAT A SMELL!
HO? YOU THINK I STINK? YOU'RE PROBABLY RIGHT.
PHHUTT!
ZZZZZZZ
NNAAA
SCOOT! VAMOOSE! AM-SCRAY! GO HOME!

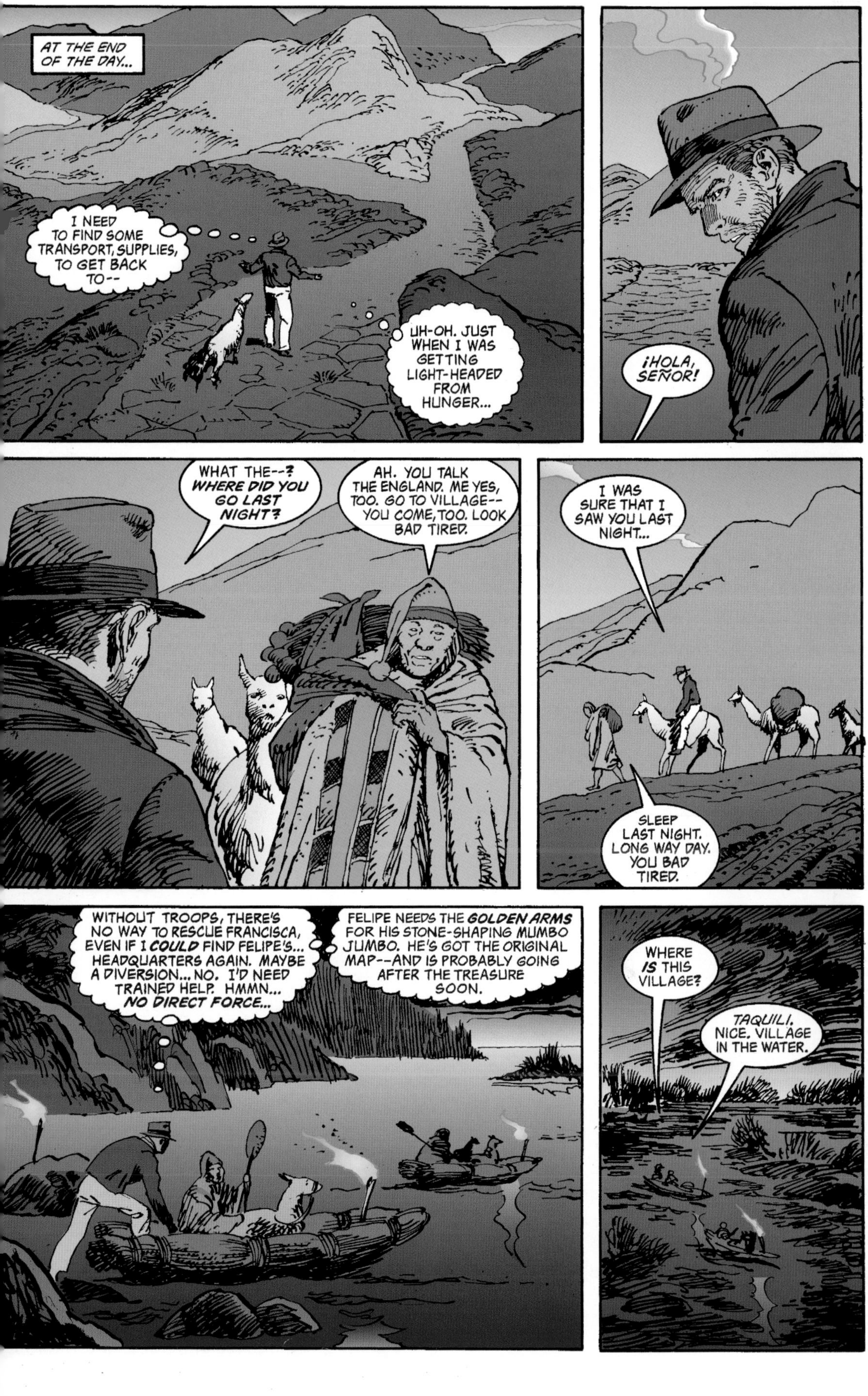
AT THE END OF THE DAY...
I NEED TO FIND SOME TRANSPORT, SUPPLIES, TO GET BACK TO--
UH-OH. JUST WHEN I WAS GETTING LIGHT-HEADED FROM HUNGER...
¡HOLA, SEÑOR!
WHAT THE--? WHERE DID YOU GO LAST NIGHT?
AH. YOU TALK THE ENGLAND. ME YES, TOO. GO TO VILLAGE-- YOU COME, TOO. LOOK BAD TIRED.
I WAS SURE THAT I SAW YOU LAST NIGHT...
SLEEP LAST NIGHT. LONG WAY DAY. YOU BAD TIRED.
WITHOUT TROOPS, THERE'S NO WAY TO RESCUE FRANCISCA, EVEN IF I COULD FIND FELIPE'S... HEADQUARTERS AGAIN. MAYBE A DIVERSION... NO. I'D NEED TRAINED HELP. HMMN... NO DIRECT FORCE...
FELIPE NEEDS THE GOLDEN ARMS FOR HIS STONE-SHAPING MUMBO JUMBO. HE'S GOT THE ORIGINAL MAP--AND IS PROBABLY GOING AFTER THE TREASURE SOON.
WHERE IS THIS VILLAGE?
TAQUILI. NICE. VILLAGE IN THE WATER.

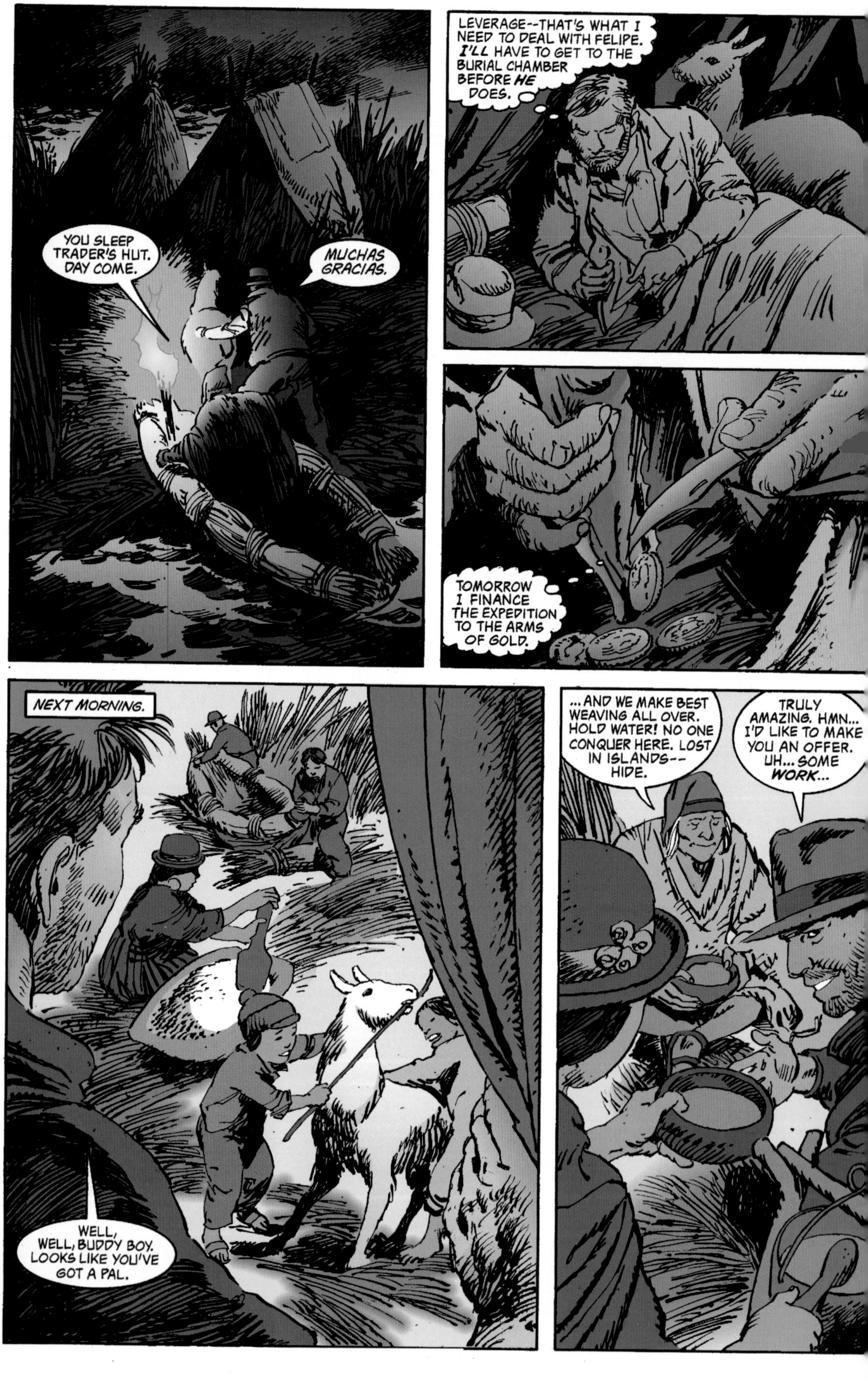
YOU SLEEP TRADER'S HUT. DAY COME.
MUCHAS GRACIAS.
LEVERAGE--THAT'S WHAT I NEED TO DEAL WITH FELIPE. I'LL HAVE TO GET TO THE BURIAL CHAMBER BEFORE HE DOES.
TOMORROW I FINANCE THE EXPEDITION TO THE ARMS OF GOLD.
NEXT MORNING.
WELL, WELL, BUDDY BOY. LOOKS LIKE YOU'VE GOT A PAL.
...AND WE MAKE BEST WEAVING ALL OVER. HOLD WATER! NO ONE CONQUER HERE. LOST IN ISLANDS-- HIDE.
TRULY AMAZING. HMN... I'D LIKE TO MAKE YOU AN OFFER. UH... SOME WORK...

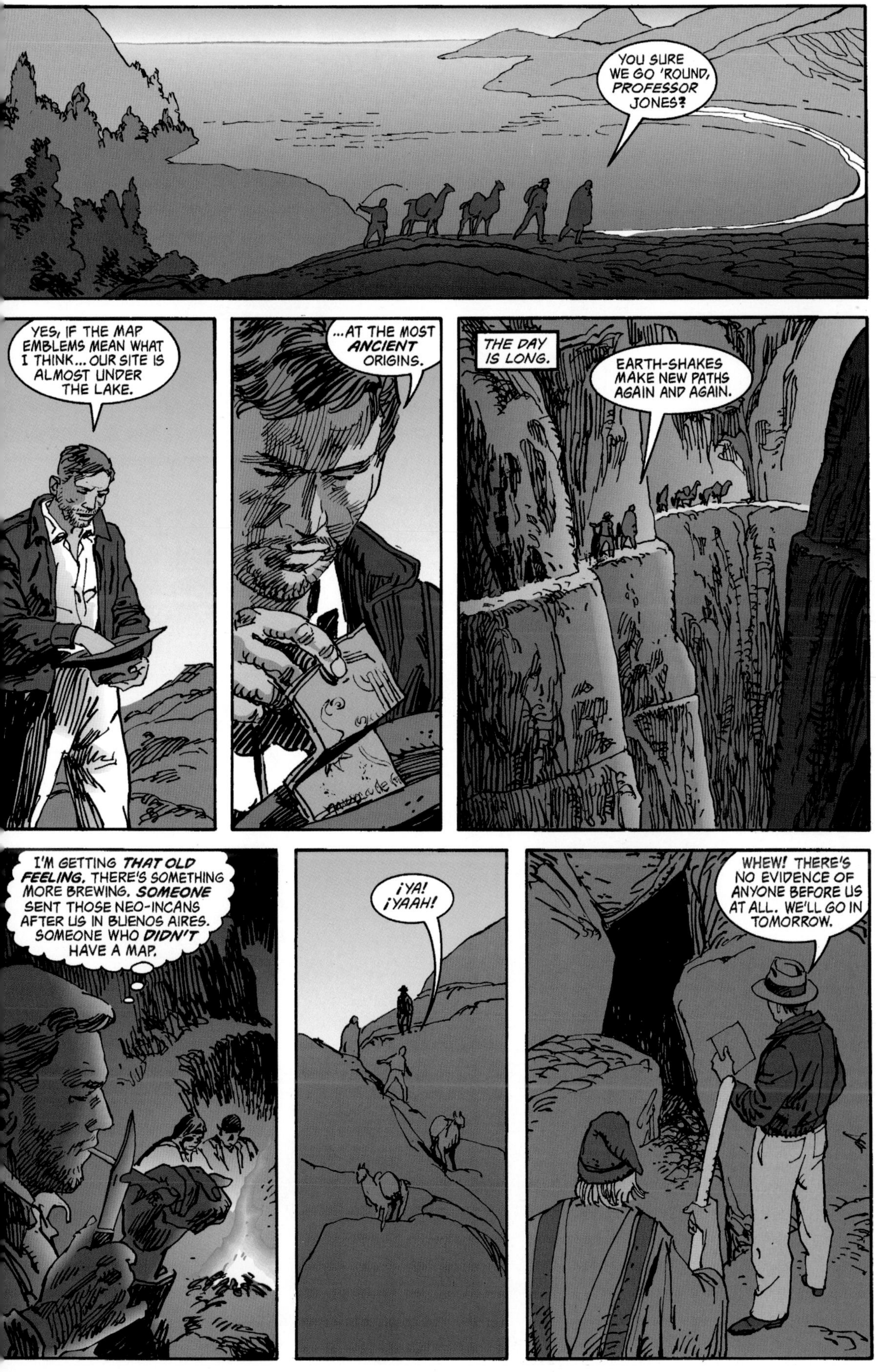
YOU SURE WE GO 'ROUND, PROFESSOR JONES?
YES, IF THE MAP EMBLEMS MEAN WHAT I THINK... OUR SITE IS ALMOST UNDER THE LAKE.
...AT THE MOST ANCIENT ORIGINS.
THE DAY IS LONG.
EARTH-SHAKES MAKE NEW PATHS AGAIN AND AGAIN.
I'M GETTING THAT OLD FEELING. THERE'S SOMETHING MORE BREWING. SOMEONE SENT THOSE NEO-INCANS AFTER US IN BUENOS AIRES. SOMEONE WHO DIDN'T HAVE A MAP.
¡YA! ¡YAAH!
WHEW! THERE'S NO EVIDENCE OF ANYONE BEFORE US AT ALL. WE'LL GO IN TOMORROW.

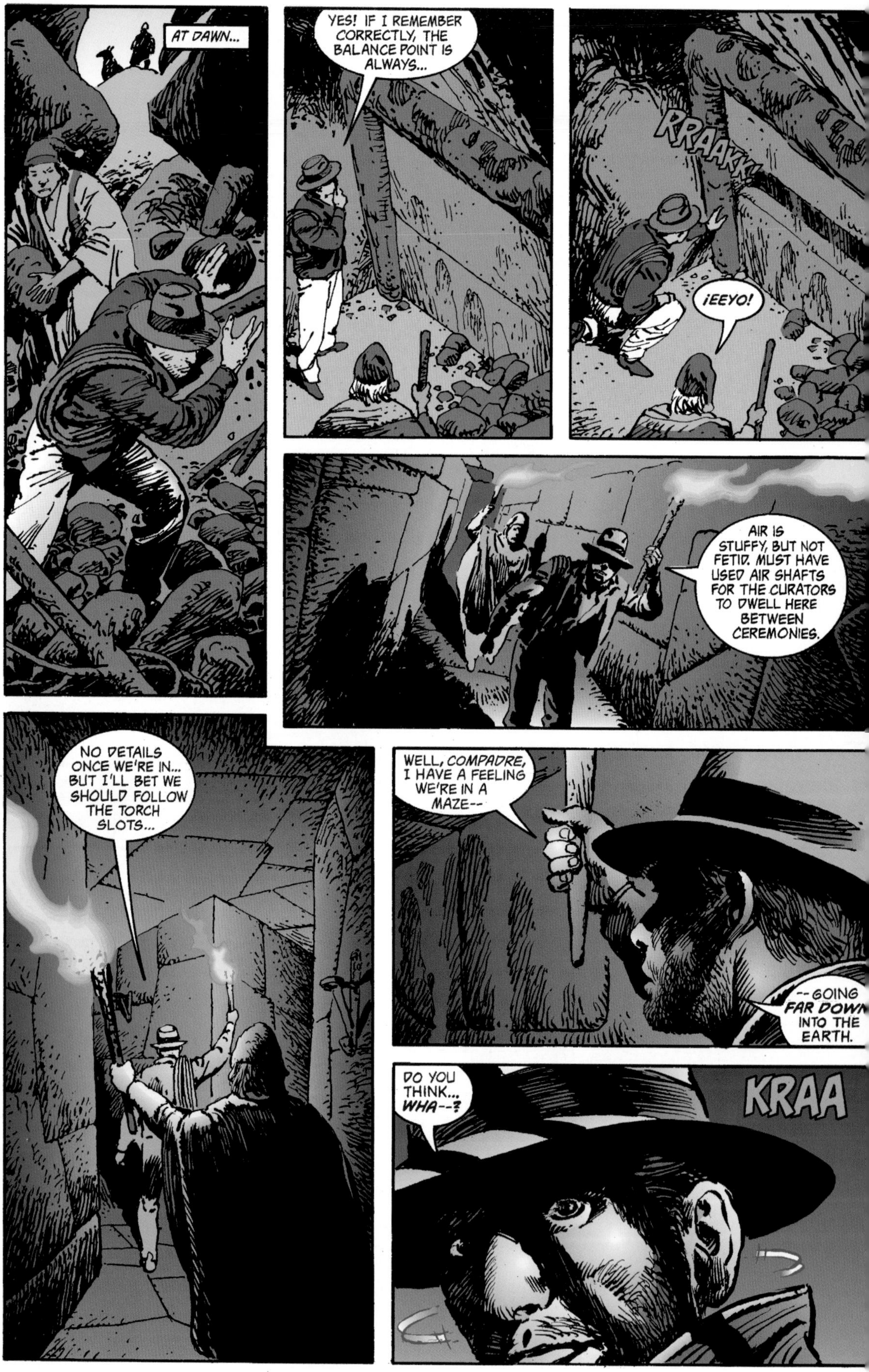

AT DAWN...
YES! IF I REMEMBER CORRECTLY, THE BALANCE POINT IS ALWAYS...
RRAAKK
¡EEYO!
AIR IS STUFFY, BUT NOT FETID. MUST HAVE USED AIR SHAFTS FOR THE CURATORS TO DWELL HERE BETWEEN CEREMONIES.
NO DETAILS ONCE WE'RE IN... BUT I'LL BET WE SHOULD FOLLOW THE TORCH SLOTS...
WELL, COMPADRE, I HAVE A FEELING WE'RE IN A MAZE--
--GOING FAR DOWN INTO THE EARTH.
DO YOU THINK... WHA--?
KRAA

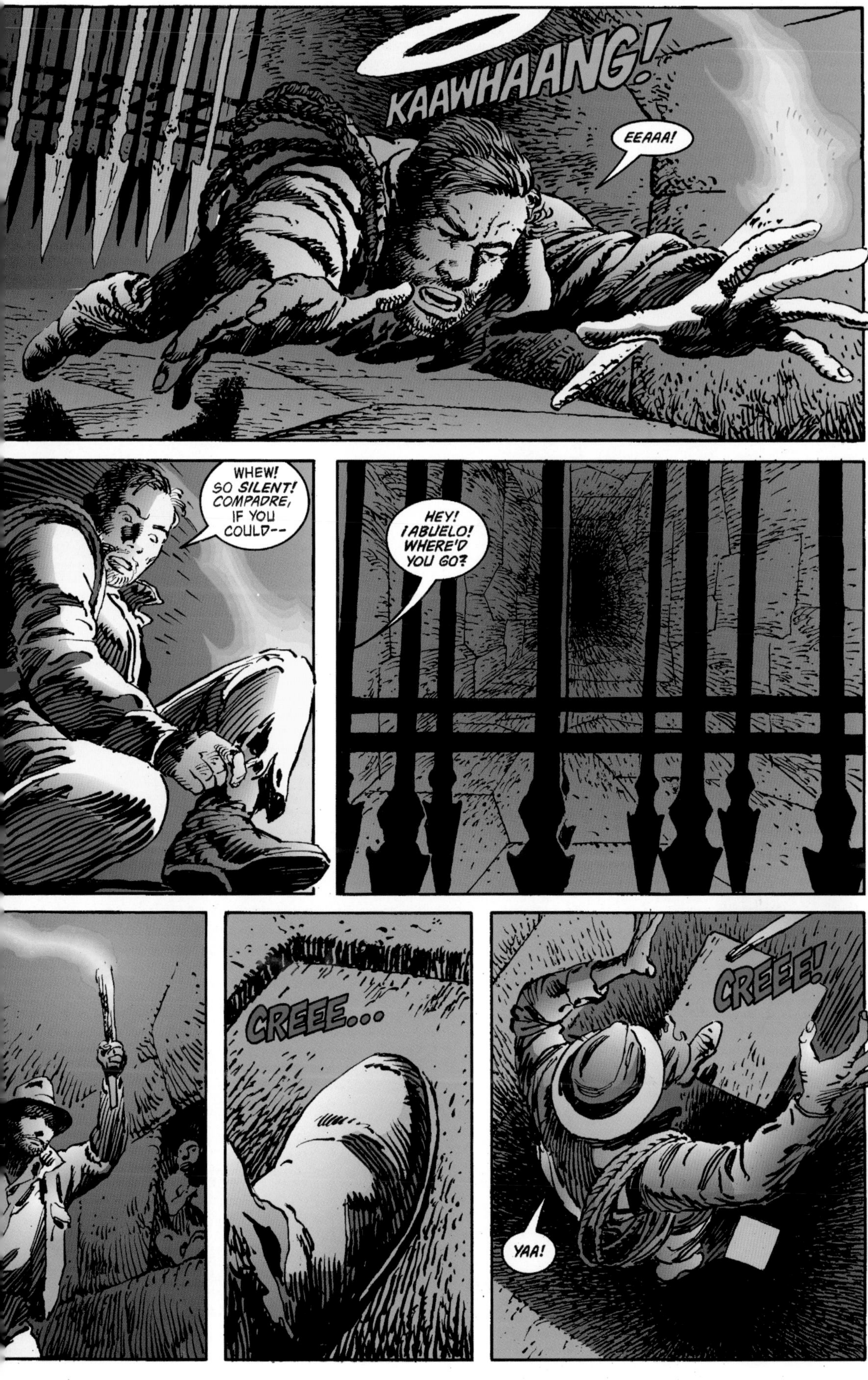
KAAWHAANG!
EEAAA!
WHEW! SO SILENT! COMPADRE, IF YOU COULD--
HEY! ¡ABUELO! WHERE'D YOU GO?
CREEE...
CREEE!
YAA!

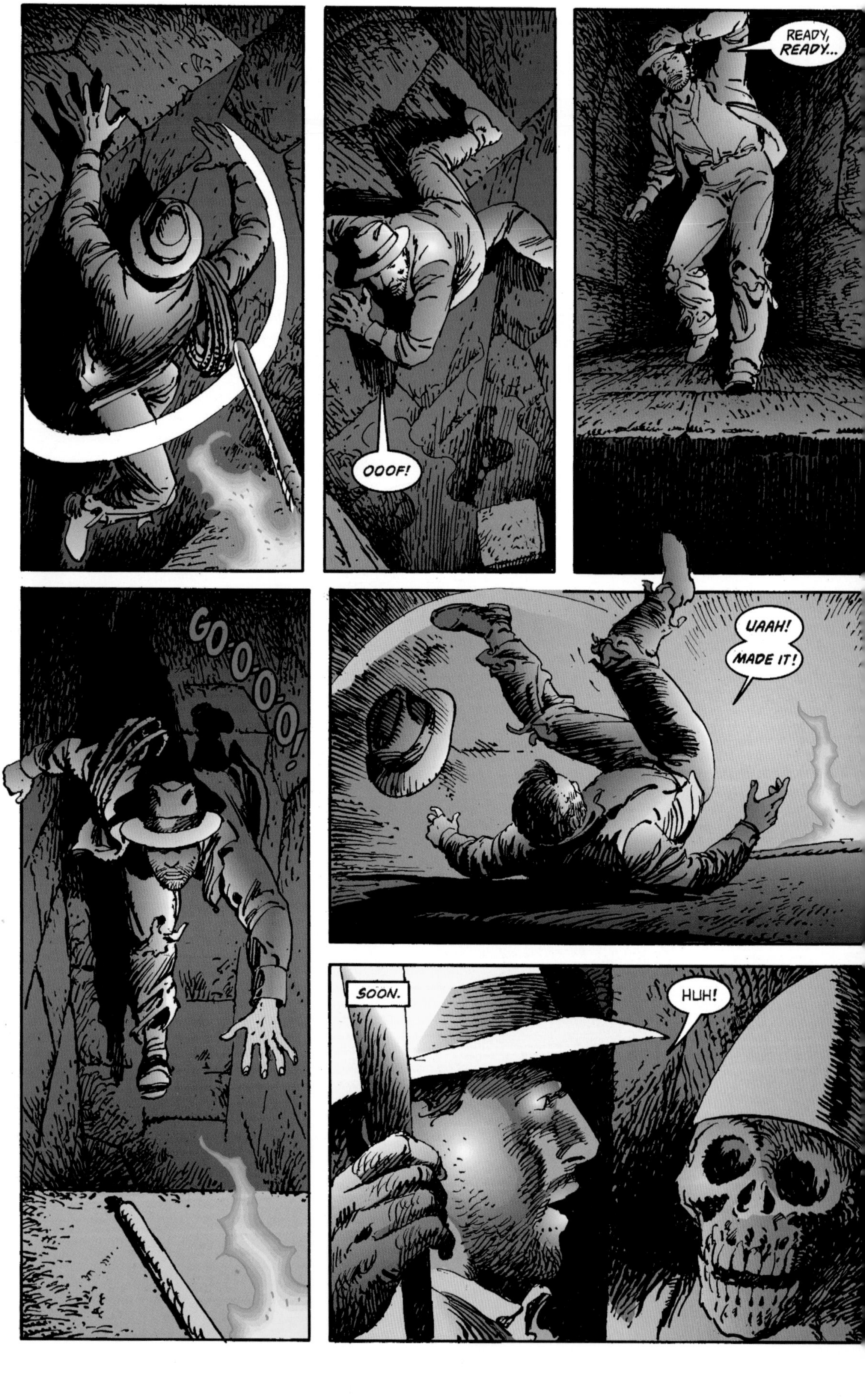
OOOF!
READY, READY...
GO-O-O-O-O!
UAAH!
MADE IT!
SOON.
HUH!

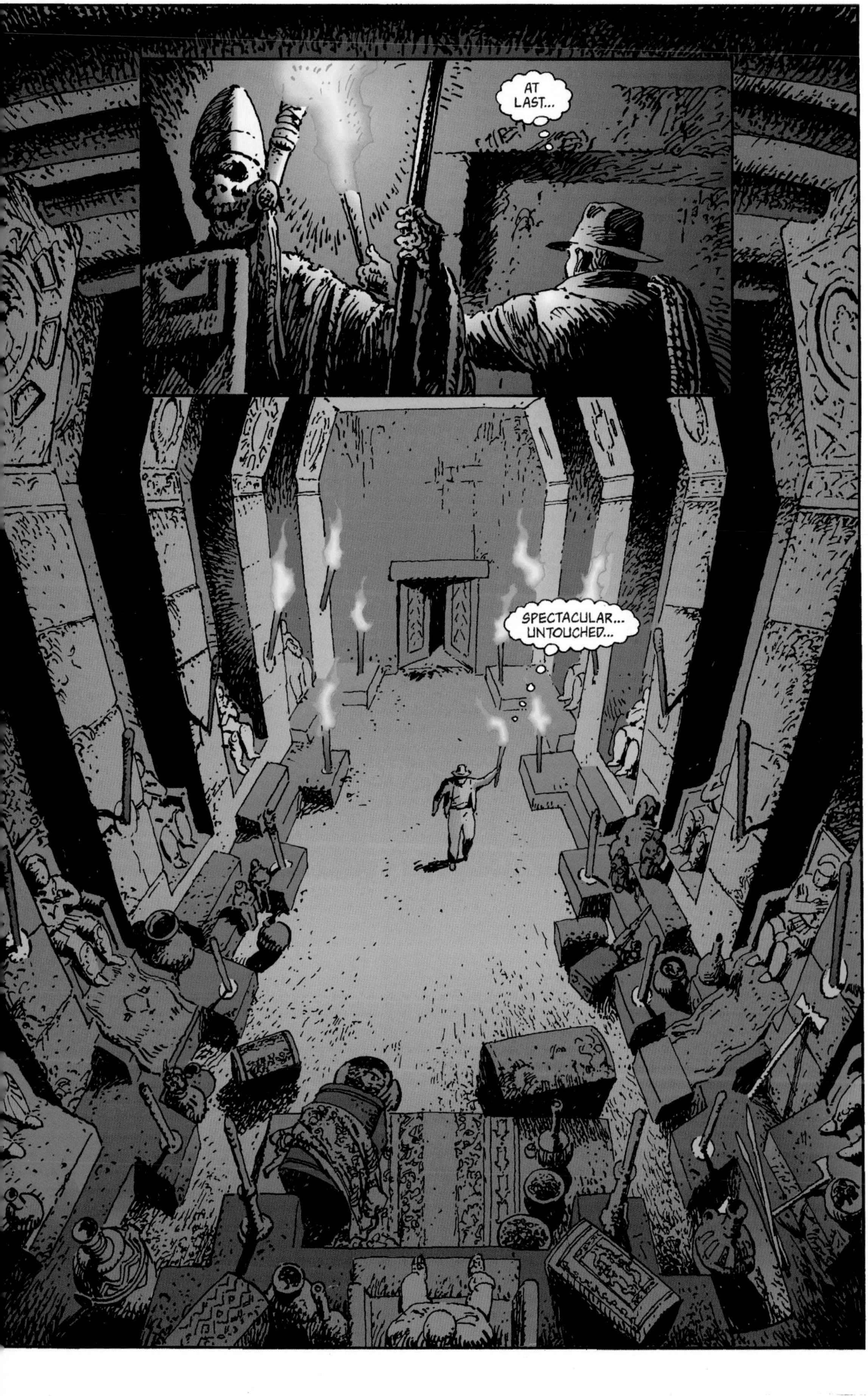
AT LAST...
SPECTACULAR... UNTOUCHED...

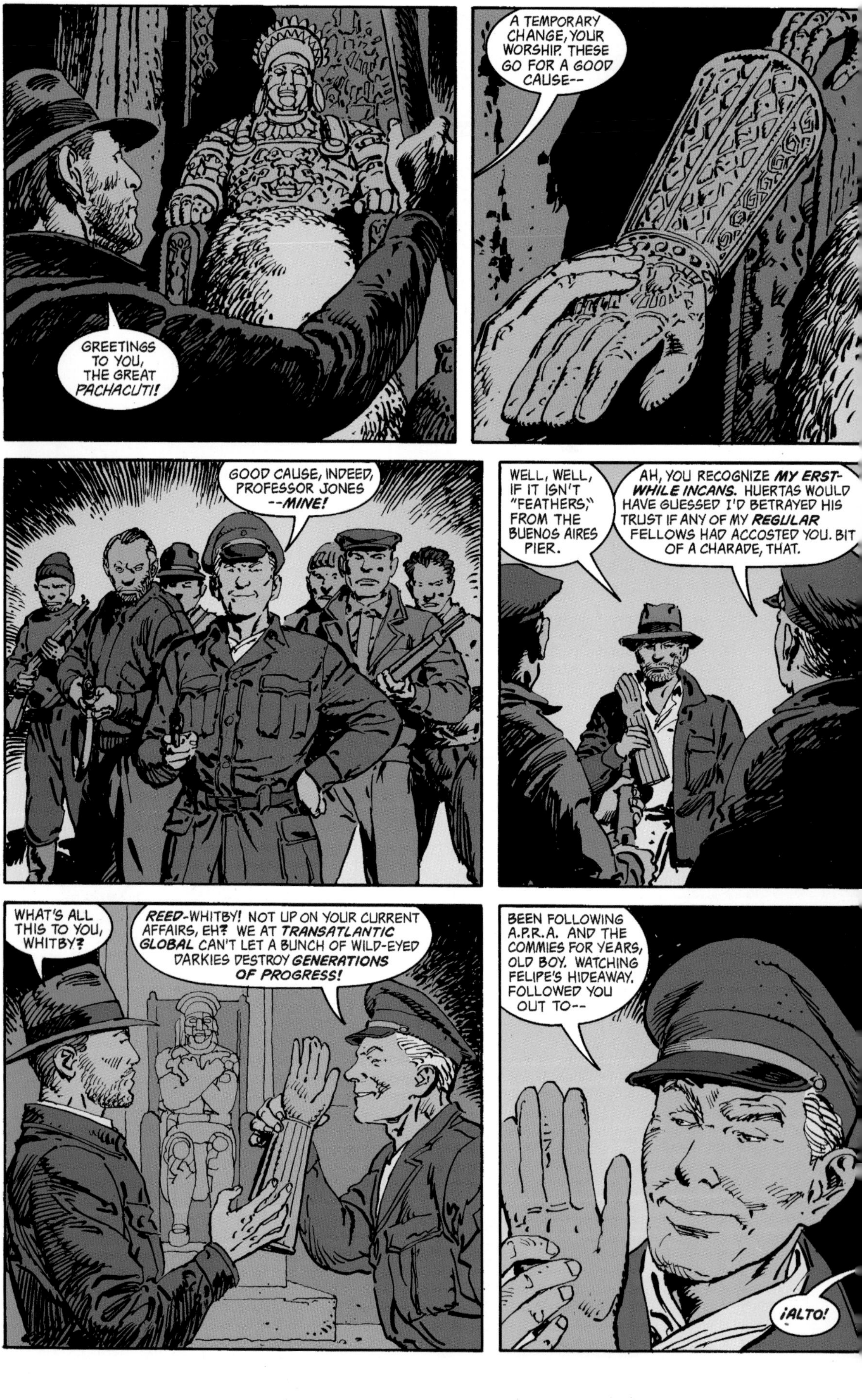
GREETINGS TO YOU, THE GREAT PACHACUTI!
A TEMPORARY CHANGE, YOUR WORSHIP. THESE GO FOR A GOOD CAUSE--
GOOD CAUSE, INDEED, PROFESSOR JONES --MINE!
WELL, WELL, IF IT ISN'T "FEATHERS," FROM THE BUENOS AIRES PIER.
AH, YOU RECOGNIZE MY ERST-WHILE INCANS. HUERTAS WOULD HAVE GUESSED I'D BETRAYED HIS TRUST IF ANY OF MY REGULAR FELLOWS HAD ACCOSTED YOU. BIT OF A CHARADE, THAT.
WHAT'S ALL THIS TO YOU, WHITBY?
REED-WHITBY! NOT UP ON YOUR CURRENT AFFAIRS, EH? WE AT TRANSATLANTIC GLOBAL CAN'T LET A BUNCH OF WILD-EYED DARKIES DESTROY GENERATIONS OF PROGRESS!
BEEN FOLLOWING A.P.R.A. AND THE COMMIES FOR YEARS, OLD BOY. WATCHING FELIPE'S HIDEAWAY. FOLLOWED YOU OUT TO--
¡ALTO!

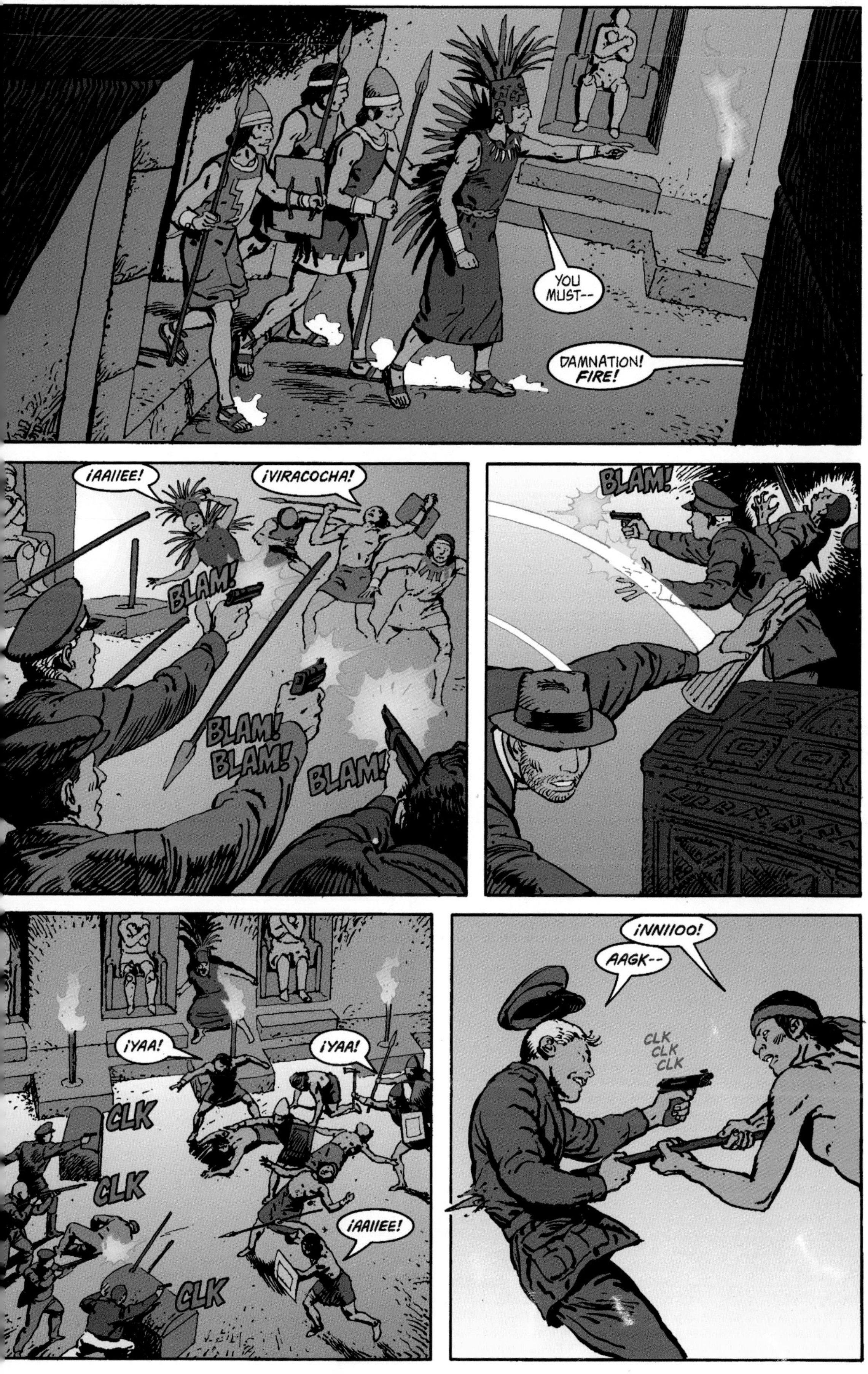
YOU MUST--
DAMNATION! FIRE!
¡AAIIEE!
¡VIRACOCHA!
BLAM!
BLAM! BLAM!
BLAM!
BLAM!
¡YAA!
¡YAA!
CLK
CLK
¡AAIIEE!
CLK
¡NNIIOO!
AAGK--
CLK CLK CLK

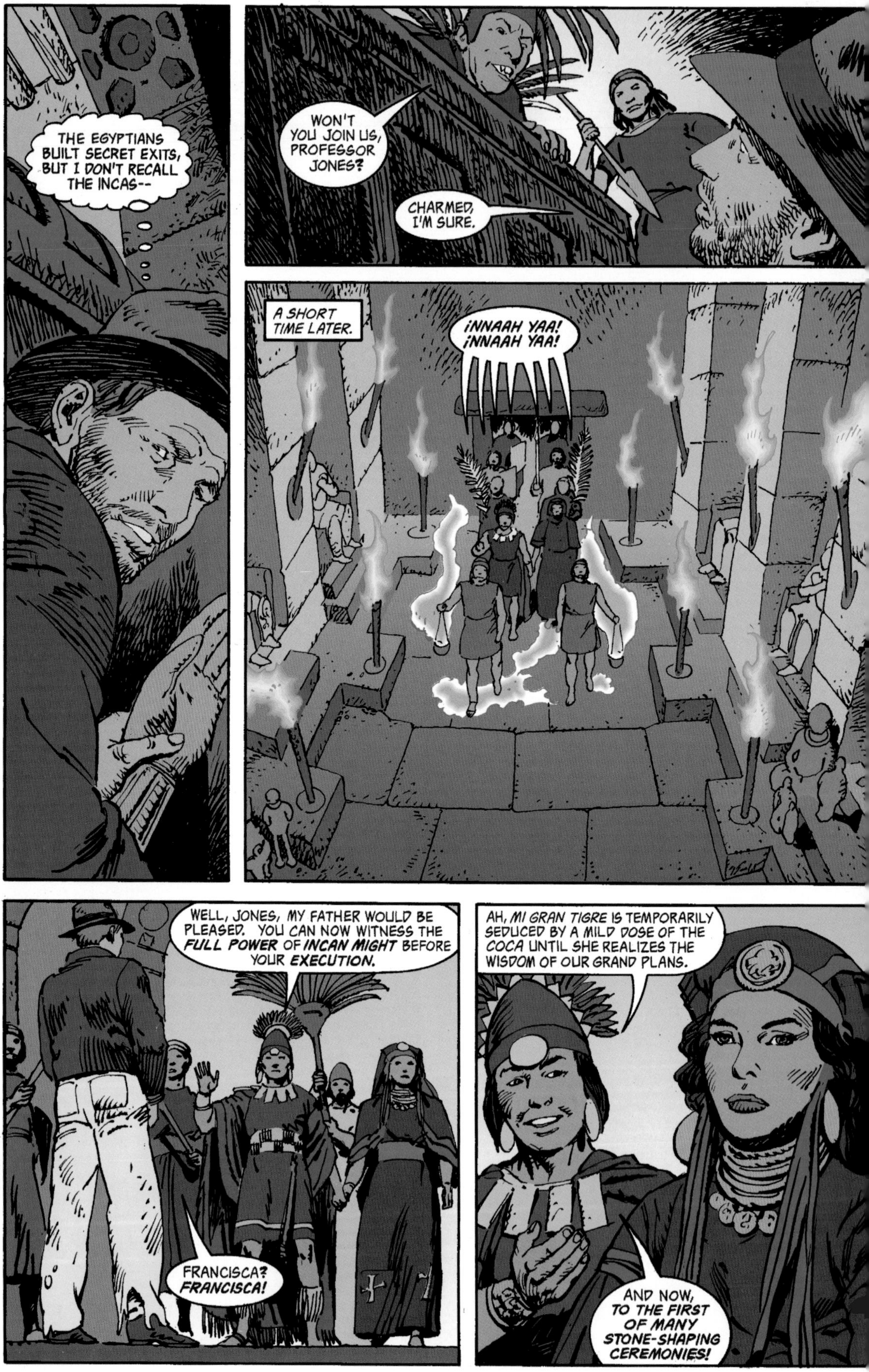
THE EGYPTIANS BUILT SECRET EXITS, BUT I DON'T RECALL THE INCAS--
WON'T YOU JOIN US, PROFESSOR JONES?
CHARMED, I'M SURE.
A SHORT TIME LATER.
¡INNAAH YAA! ¡INNAAH YAA!
WELL, JONES, MY FATHER WOULD BE PLEASED. YOU CAN NOW WITNESS THE FULL POWER OF INCAN MIGHT BEFORE YOUR EXECUTION.
FRANCISCA? FRANCISCA!
AH, MI GRAN TIGRE IS TEMPORARILY SEDUCED BY A MILD DOSE OF THE COCA UNTIL SHE REALIZES THE WISDOM OF OUR GRAND PLANS.
AND NOW, TO THE FIRST OF MANY STONE-SHAPING CEREMONIES!

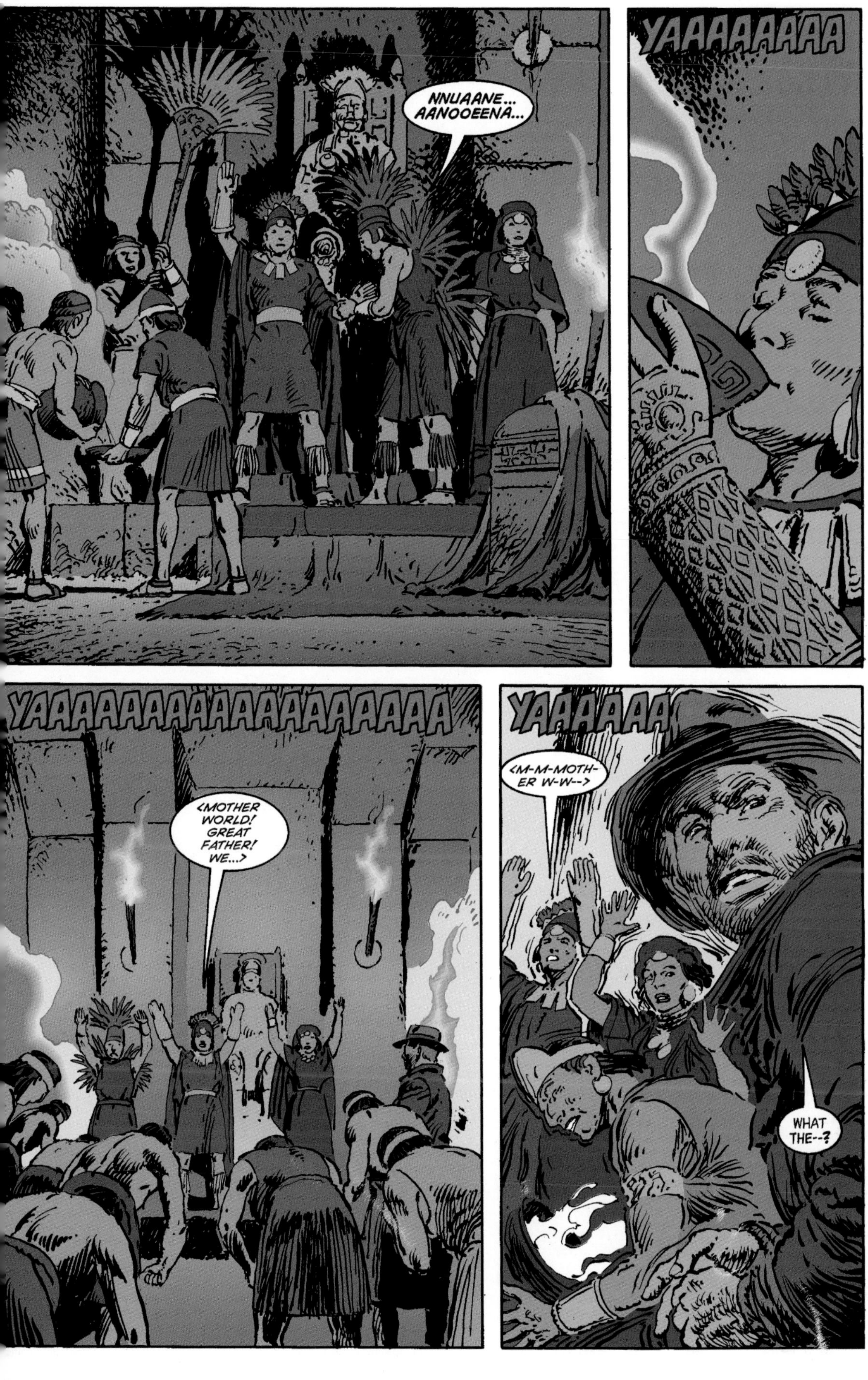

NNUAANE... AANOOEENA...
YAAAAAAAA
YAAAAAAAAAAAAAAAAAA
<MOTHER WORLD! GREAT FATHER! WE...>
YAAAAAA
<M-M-MOTH-ER W-W-->
WHAT THE--?

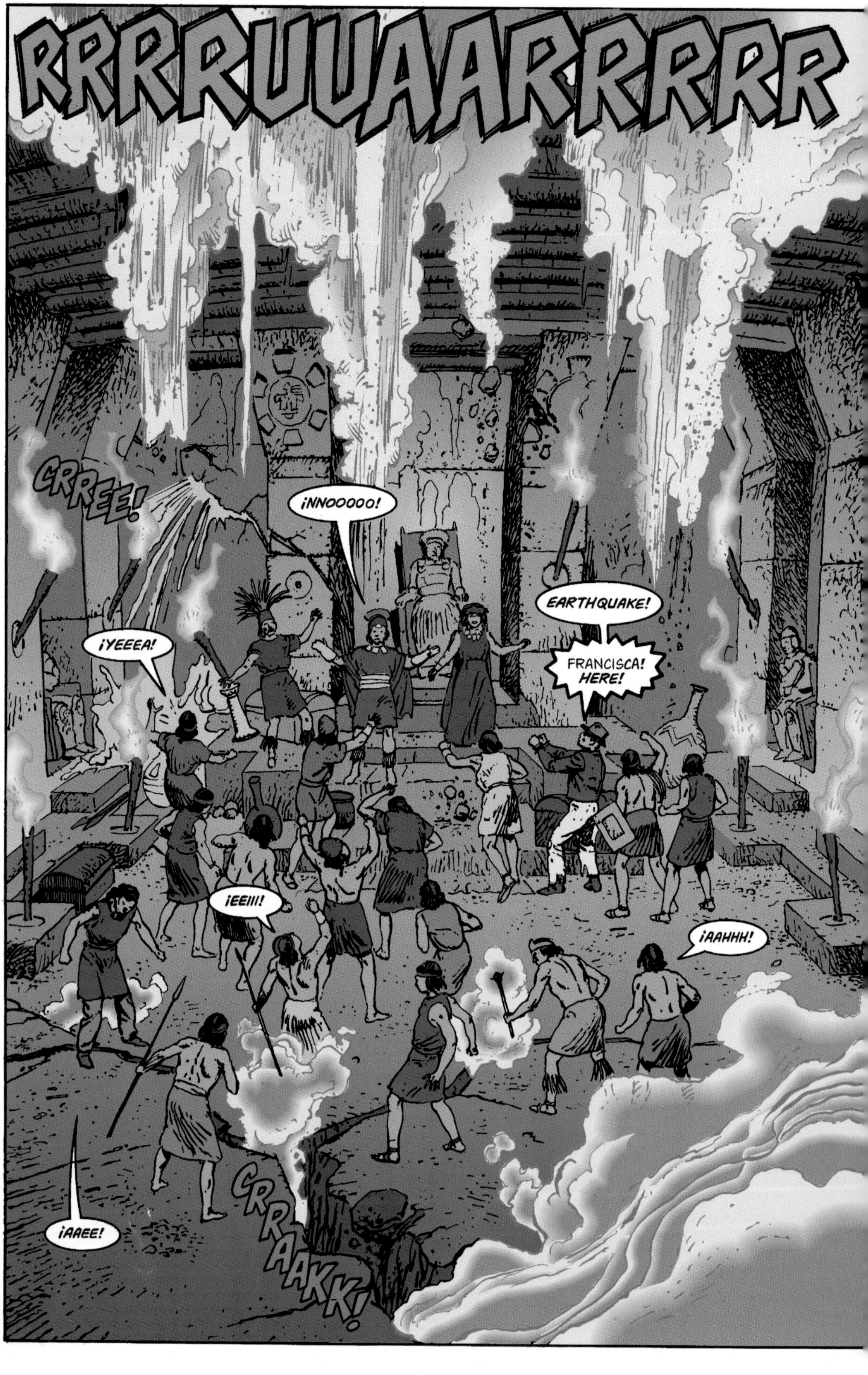
RRRRUUAARRRRR
CRREE!
¡NNOOOOO!
EARTHQUAKE!
¡YEEEA!
FRANCISCA! HERE!
¡EEIII!
¡AAHHH!
¡AAEE!
CRRAAKK!

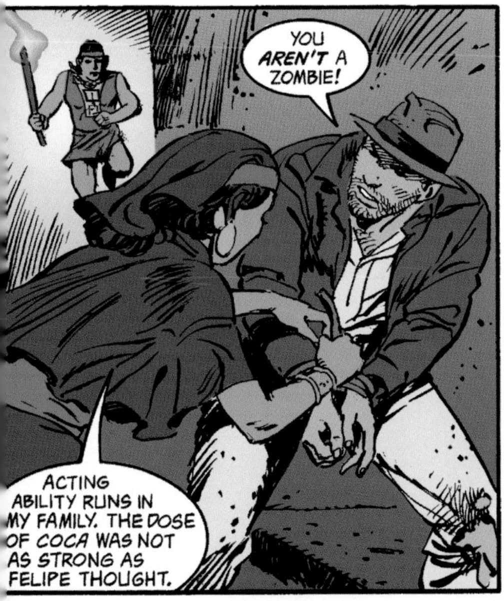

YOU AREN'T A ZOMBIE!
ACTING ABILITY RUNS IN MY FAMILY. THE DOSE OF COCA WAS NOT AS STRONG AS FELIPE THOUGHT.

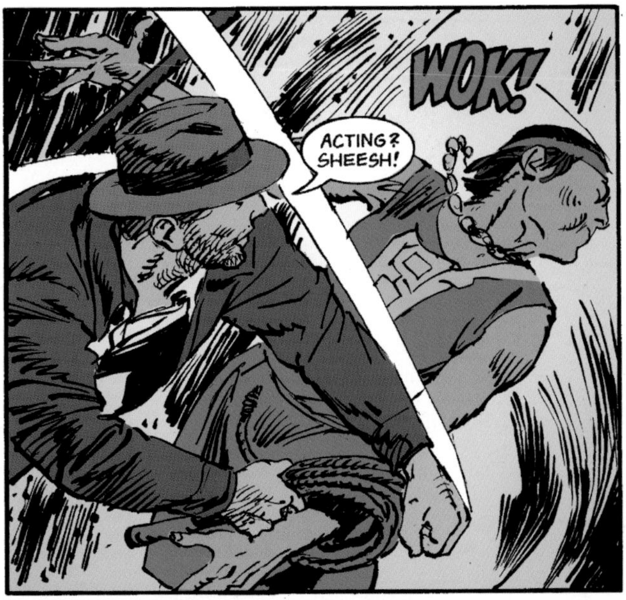

WOK!
ACTING? SHEESH!

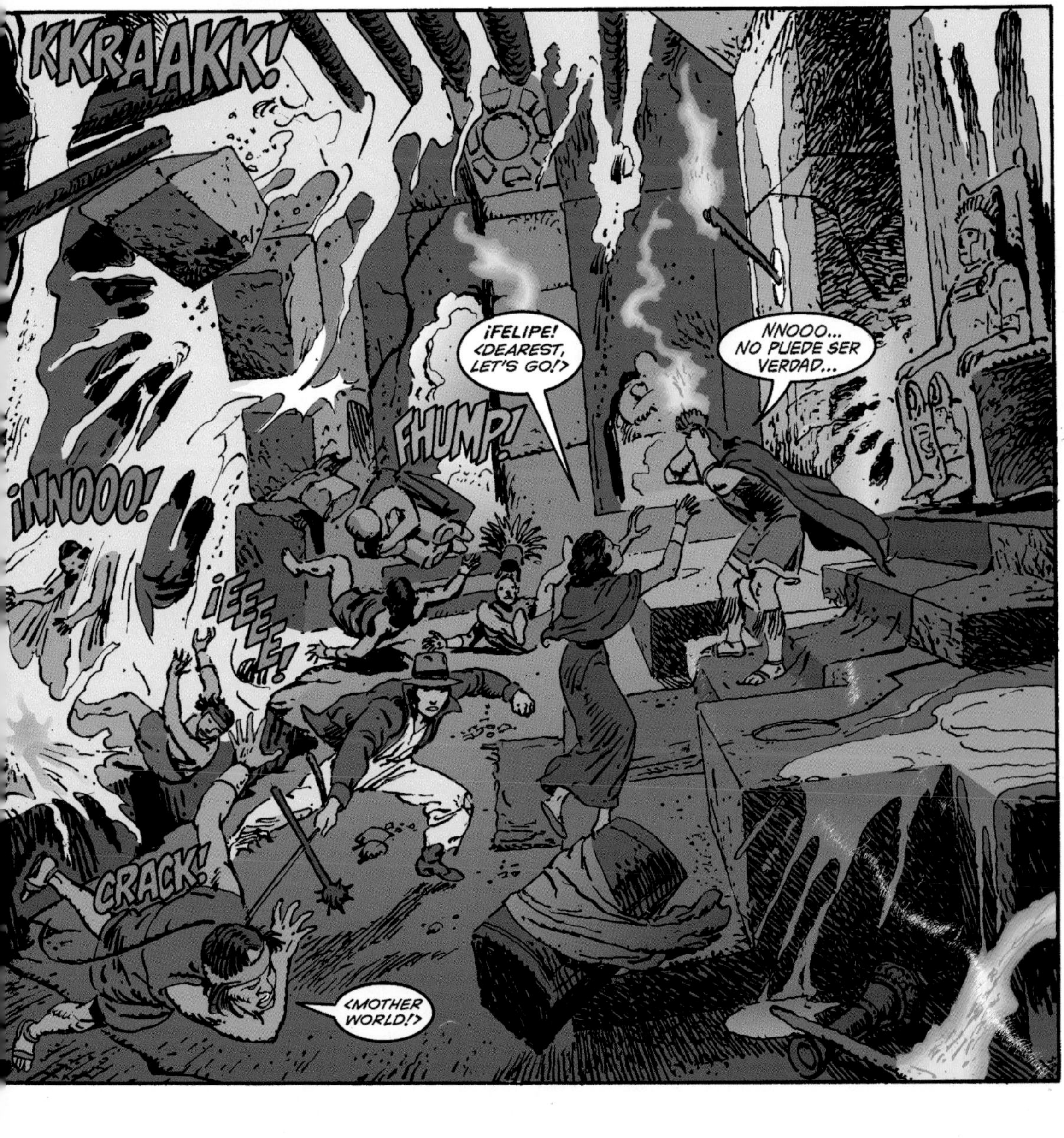

KKRAAKK!
¡FELIPE! <DEAREST, LET'S GO!>
NNOOO... NO PUEDE SER VERDAD...
FHUMP!
¡NNOOO!
¡EEEE!
CRACK!
<MOTHER WORLD!>

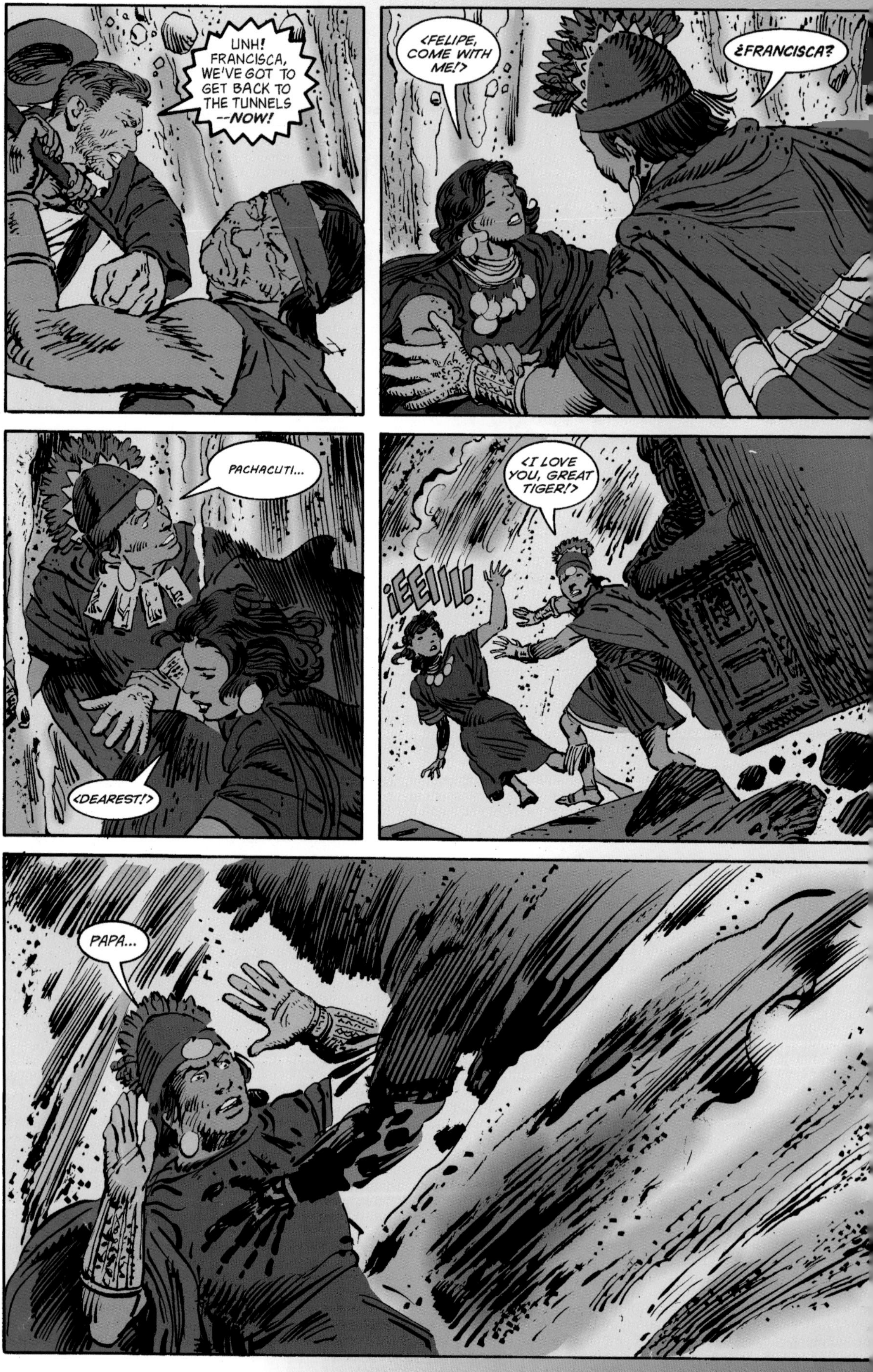
UNH! FRANCISCA, WE'VE GOT TO GET BACK TO THE TUNNELS --NOW!
<FELIPE, COME WITH ME!>
¿FRANCISCA?
PACHACUTI...
<DEAREST!>
<I LOVE YOU, GREAT TIGER!>
¡EEIII!
PAPA...

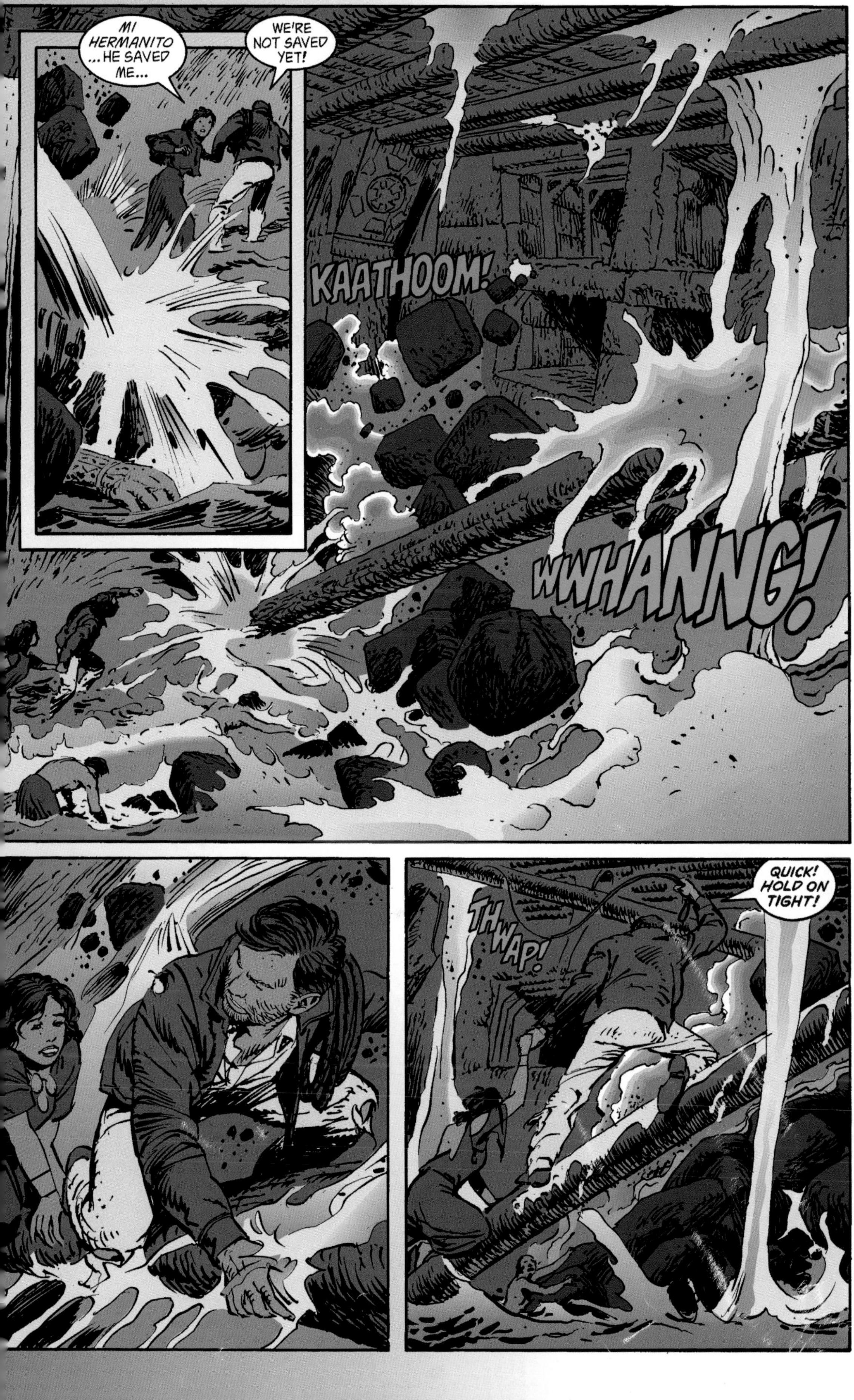
MI HERMANITO ...HE SAVED ME...
WE'RE NOT SAVED YET!
KAATHOOM!
WWHANNG!
THWAP!
QUICK! HOLD ON TIGHT!

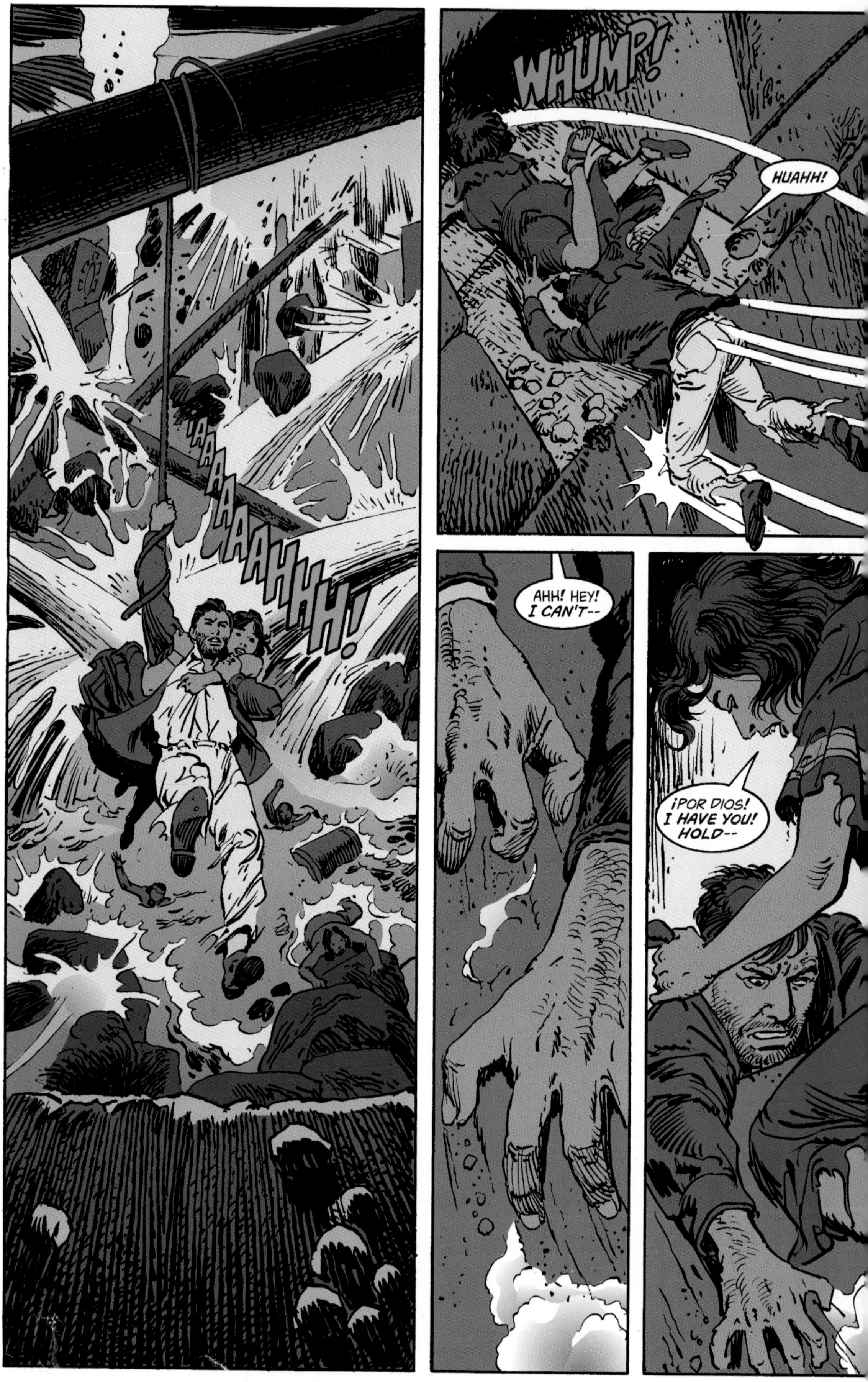
AAAAAAAAAHHH!
WHUMP!
HUAHH!
AHH! HEY! I CAN'T--
¡POR DIOS! I HAVE YOU! HOLD--

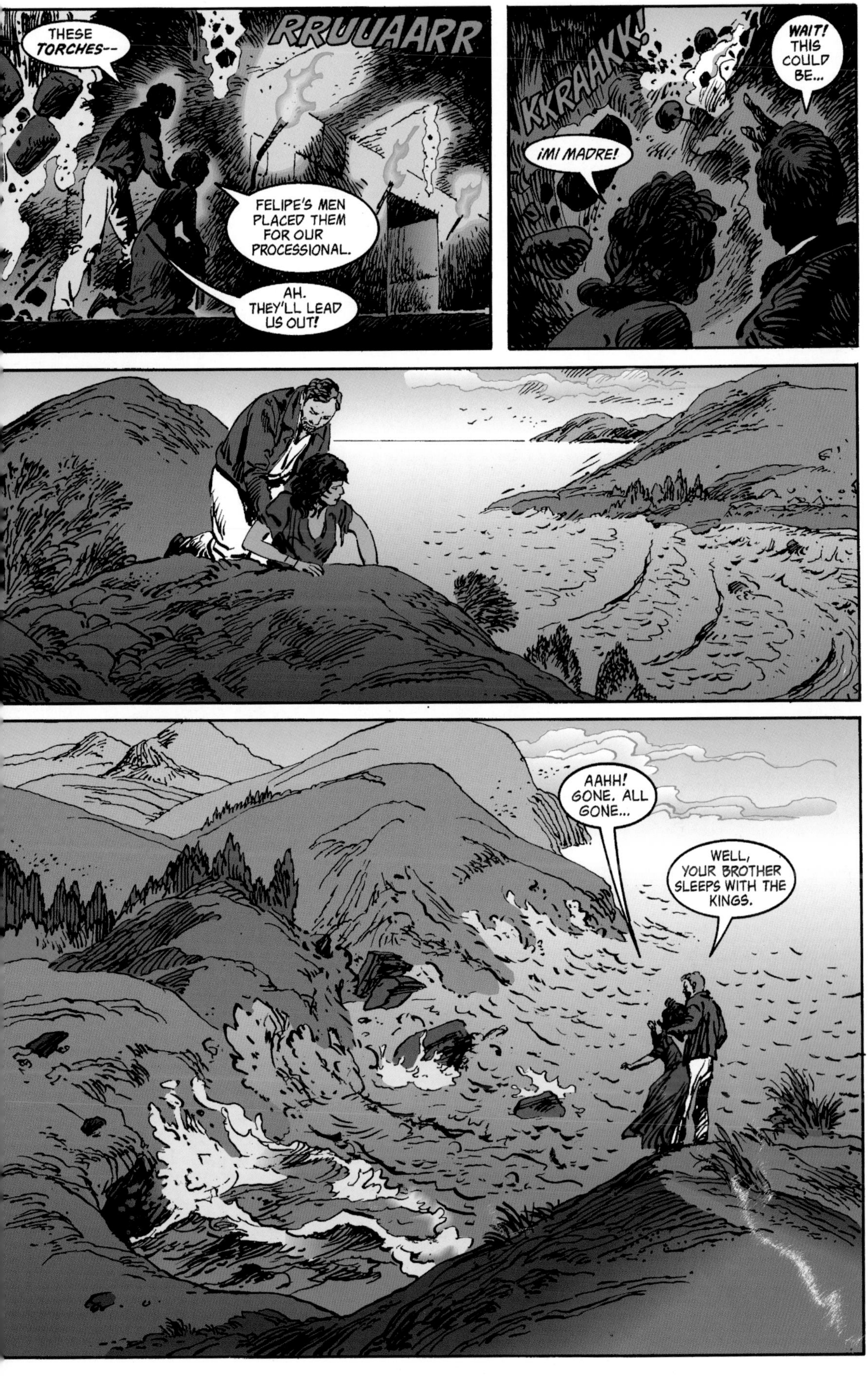

RRUUAARR
THESE TORCHES--
FELIPE'S MEN PLACED THEM FOR OUR PROCESSIONAL.
AH. THEY'LL LEAD US OUT!
KKRAAKK!
WAIT! THIS COULD BE...
¡MI MADRE!
AAHH! GONE. ALL GONE...
WELL, YOUR BROTHER SLEEPS WITH THE KINGS.

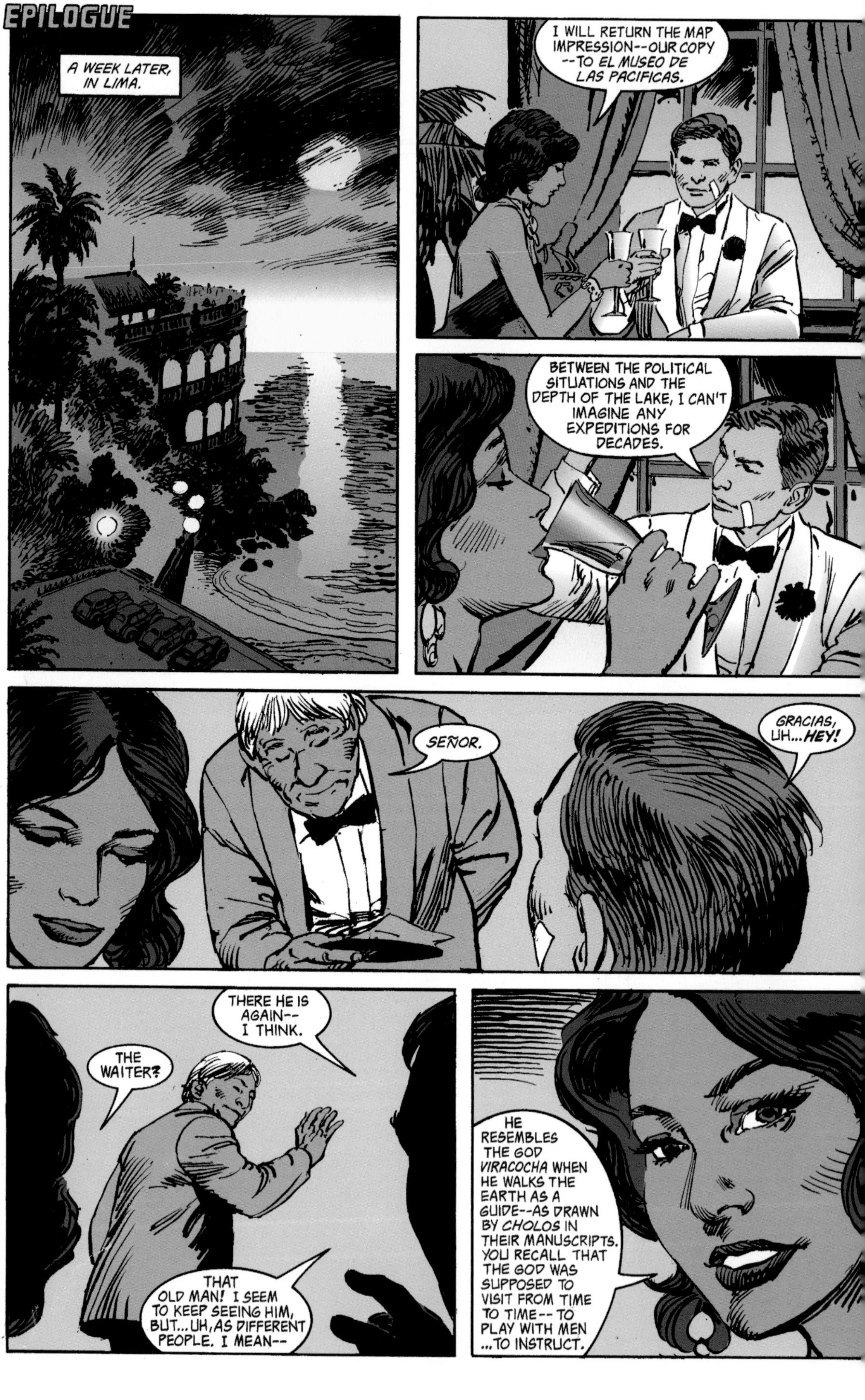
EPILOGUE
A WEEK LATER, IN LIMA.
I WILL RETURN THE MAP IMPRESSION--OUR COPY --TO EL MUSEO DE LAS PACIFICAS.
BETWEEN THE POLITICAL SITUATIONS AND THE DEPTH OF THE LAKE, I CAN'T IMAGINE ANY EXPEDITIONS FOR DECADES.
SEÑOR.
GRACIAS, UH... HEY!
THERE HE IS AGAIN-- I THINK.
THE WAITER?
THAT OLD MAN! I SEEM TO KEEP SEEING HIM, BUT... UH, AS DIFFERENT PEOPLE. I MEAN--
HE RESEMBLES THE GOD VIRACOCHA WHEN HE WALKS THE EARTH AS A GUIDE--AS DRAWN BY CHOLOS IN THEIR MANUSCRIPTS. YOU RECALL THAT THE GOD WAS SUPPOSED TO VISIT FROM TIME TO TIME-- TO PLAY WITH MEN ...TO INSTRUCT.

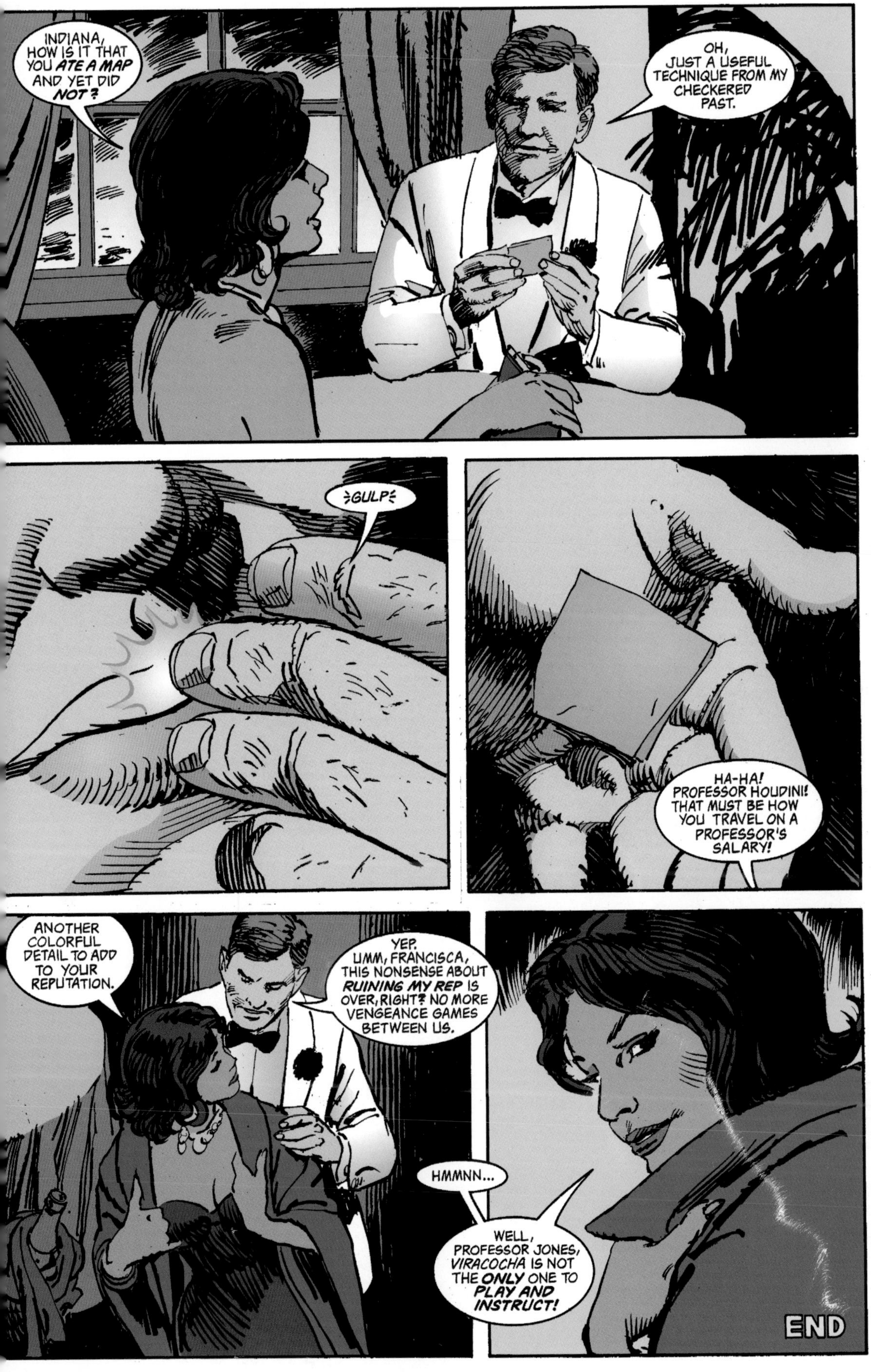
INDIANA, HOW IS IT THAT YOU ATE A MAP AND YET DID NOT?
OH, JUST A USEFUL TECHNIQUE FROM MY CHECKERED PAST.
GULP
HA-HA! PROFESSOR HOUDINI! THAT MUST BE HOW YOU TRAVEL ON A PROFESSOR'S SALARY!
ANOTHER COLORFUL DETAIL TO ADD TO YOUR REPUTATION.
YEP. UMM, FRANCISCA, THIS NONSENSE ABOUT RUINING MY REP IS OVER, RIGHT? NO MORE VENGEANCE GAMES BETWEEN US.
HMMNN...
WELL, PROFESSOR JONES, VIRACOCHA IS NOT THE ONLY ONE TO PLAY AND INSTRUCT!
END

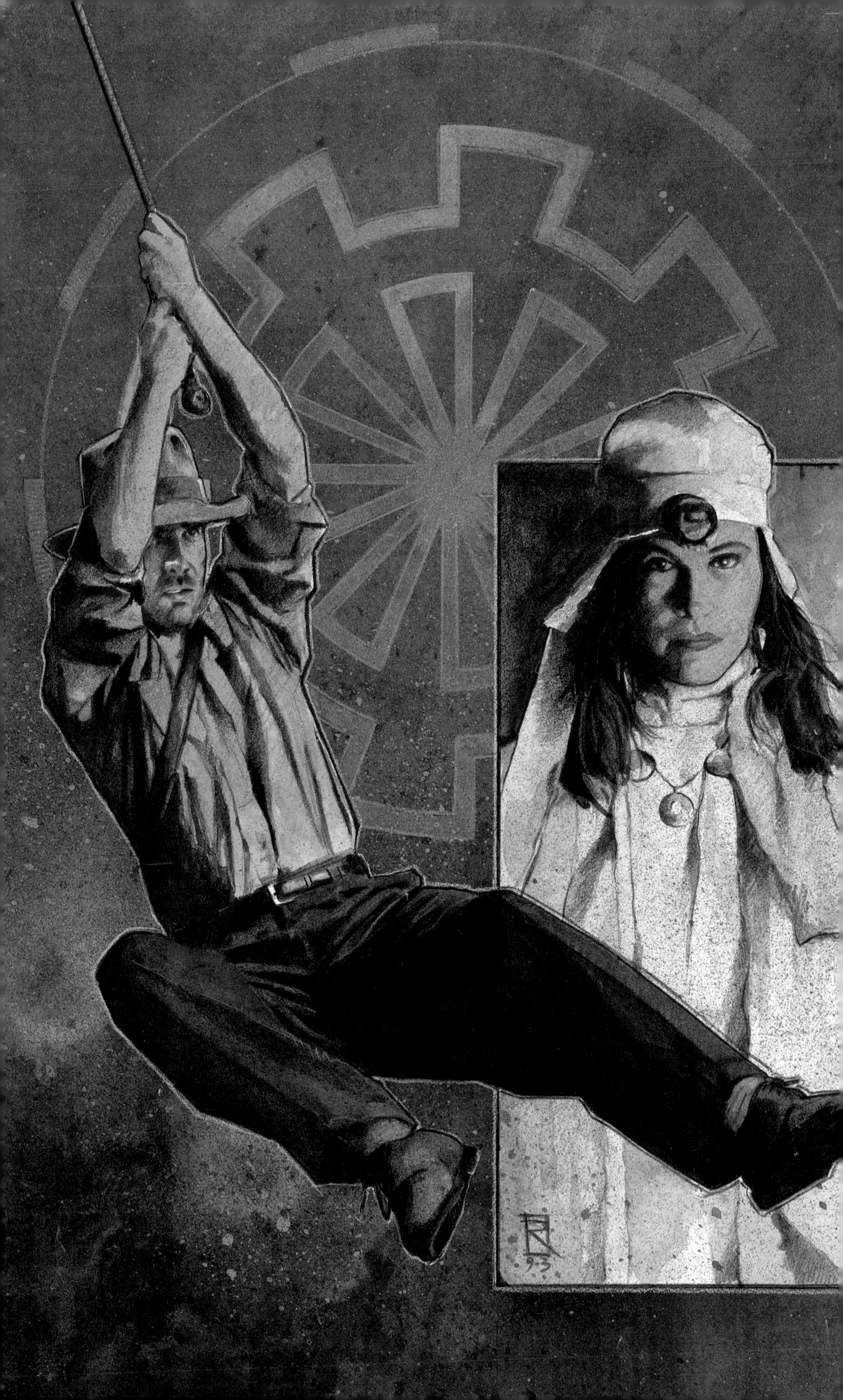